BRINE

BRINE

a novel

KATE SMITH

Two Harbors Press
Minneapolis, MN

Two Harbors Press
322 First Avenue N, 5th floor
Minneapolis, MN 55401
612.455.2293
www.TwoHarborsPress.com

brinebook.com

ISBN-13: 978-1-63505-031-8
LCCN: 2016901315

Distributed by Itasca Books

Cover Design by Alan Pranke
Typeset by A. M. Wells
Additional Cover Art: Ishmael Woodcut by Charles Ailstock

Printed in the United States of America

for my saltwater husband

"The hypothetical aquatic phase of the ancestral apes during the fossil gap would have been brief, a matter of maybe two or three million years. Nobody has suggested that they turned into mermen and mermaids."

Elaine Morgan
The Aquatic Ape Hypothesis

PROLOGUE

LET'S NOT TIPTOE AROUND IT: this is a story about mermaids.

Not a fairy tale. A true story.

My story.

I suppose I could swim up beside you to prove myself, but that would take away the mystery.

I'm a mermaid.

You're just going to have to take my word for it.

PART ONE

West Coast

1

SHE WHIPPED AROUND THE BLIND CURVE, windows down, music blaring. Beyond the guardrail, lacy waves glittered with a hint of pre-dawn light. Their fight had left her boiling.

She'd spent last night at her place, the first night back in the trailer park in almost a year. God, Nick's place was so much nicer than hers—ocean view and leather couches. Was she jealous? Maybe. The realization unsettled her. Who had she become? In the stale darkness of her cramped entryway, she'd plopped her bag on the laminate floor, not sure whether to cry or run. She had wanted to punch a wall, break a window. *Who did he think he was?*

Instead, she'd snatched paintbrushes from an old coffee jar, tugged the cord on a hanging light bulb, and thrown a blank canvas on the easel. She'd worked through the night in her trailer, braless, in overalls and a Hanes V-neck, her strawberry blond hair tied back in a messy knot. She finger-painted at times, livid reds swathed across the canvas, temperamental purple accents, sad blue undertones, wiping tears from her cheeks with messy fingers.

Her face was still streaked with paint when the Mexican border cops checked her California license that morning and waved her onward into Baja.

Screw Nicholas.

She thought about her parents' wedding, in a small chapel with only a handful of guests. How different from the wedding she and Nicholas were planning. She wondered if her mother had worn a veil; if her father had gone so far as to borrow a jacket and tie. She wondered what it would feel like to walk down the aisle with neither of them there.

If someone asked her, she would've said that she still loved Nicholas. They'd fought like this before. She was pissed off—sure as shit she was—but she was still wearing the ring.

The sun peeked out over the hills. She saw a red flannel shirt and a man waving it. An overturned eighteen-wheeler blocked the entire road, a dark gush of oil spilling from the ruptured tank, the man waving his arms frantically. She slammed the brakes, but her tires had already caught the slick.

She slid sideways, crashed through the guardrail, and plunged over the cliff.

The truck felt heavy for a split second, then became weightless. Her bag spilled across the seat and the contents—spare change, pages of her journal—hung in space for a moment as gravity lost its grip. She was falling. She glimpsed the froth beneath her, the churning blue-green rushing toward her. Then the slam of concrete water and a swarm of delicate bubbles as the truck broke through the crust of the sea.

Nothing hurt.

A hand with fingernails like talons yanked her through the window of the sinking truck and jerked her to the surface.

She coughed up water. Hands pulled off her shoes and un-buttoned her pants. She was breathing heavily, pushing the hands away, shocked and scared, but too weak to fight whoever—whatever—had her. The hands stripped her jeans and underwear, leaving her naked from the waist down. She blinked the stinging salt water from her eyes, trying to see. As soon as her eyes began to clear, she was tucked beneath the water again, the strong arm of her rescuer wrapped around her, towing her away from the scene. She watched the blur of bubbles from her sinking truck disappear. Just as her lungs felt as if they would burst, she was brought to the surface.

And then she noticed it: a warm tingling in her legs and feet she'd never felt before. The sensation was strange, painful even—like rope burn—but also mildly comforting, like a constricting embrace. Underwater, her vision had a dreamy quality. Her two legs—was this possible?—had grown together into one extension. Her eyes burned from the brine, and she pinched them shut, skeptical. But her hands needed to know what was happening, and they reached down to feel that the skin of her lower half had thickened to the texture of rubber.

She kicked and felt her feet move as one. Disbelieving, she forced her eyes open and saw, not her two legs, but the elongated and flattened form of a flipper. She choked water into her lungs and was again brought to the surface by her rescuer. She belched and coughed; water streamed down her face. Her savior cooed and petted her hair with a clawed hand.

Her eyes finally cleared, and she was looking into a woman's eyes. Intelligent eyes. But was this a human? Could a human swim as fast as they had just swam?

A finger pressed its way into her mouth. She clamped down on the rough flesh, but the salty finger did not flinch. A gritty substance was rubbed into her gums, and immediately she felt drowsy as the bitter paste melted on her tongue. She felt the rocking of her body as she floated on a bed of kelp bulbs and the daunting swirl of creatures swimming all around her. She sensed the sheer heaviness of her legs: so heavy that when she tried to lift them, she realized they were the thick skin of a tail. She compelled her mind to stay alert but couldn't resist the bliss of soft, downy sleep.

2

IT WAS DARK WHEN SHE FULLY AWOKE, disoriented. The sky above her was a sea of stars despite the glow from the round, milky moon. Muscles in her neck strained taut as she lifted her head. Her legs were back.

No way. Not possible.

She dropped her head. She could smell the ocean now, bitter and healing, like the amber blotch of iodine rubbed on her chin once after falling off the monkey bars. Higher in her nasal cavity, she caught the acrid stench of dried fish blood. She felt the soggy blanket of nets beneath her. She was in the bottom of a boat.

A man had found her on a beach: the flashback drifted in, strange and yet pronounced. The man—he'd pinched her cheeks to force her mouth open, poured fresh water from his canteen onto her face. She recalled him wrapping his long, bony fingers around a worn rubber tiller. She remembered how he'd watched the waves with knowing eyes, timing his approach between the swell lines. She'd heard him gun the motor and then the two of them were lifted, revved forward on the back of a wave, riding a hump of water to the beach. He'd cut the motor and lifted the propeller out of the sand just before the hull scraped the gritty shore. A lone gull squawked overhead as soon as the boat stopped, laughing down at her.

The man mumbled. She'd felt the boat shift, felt him struggle to get out. Where were they? She heard the man's irregular footsteps limping away. Was he just leaving her there? She could feel the prickly pinkness of her sunburned skin. Hadn't it been a woman who rescued her? Who was this man? But even beneath the blinding white of the blazing sun, it was too easy to slip back under, to surrender to the grogginess. Her lids closed mechanically and locked like garage doors.

Now it was dark. How long had she been here? She twitched her toes, opened and closed her fists a few times. Everything seemed intact. No broken bones. Exhaustion, but no pain. She reached for the side of the boat to lift her body to sitting. A muttering voice in the distance froze her movements. The man's voice grew closer, approaching. Without a sound, she nestled back in the nets, perked her ears.

The footsteps came within a few feet of the boat, and with them, a miasma of tequila. The mumbling ceased, and she heard the unzipping of pants, the fumble of clothing. A dribble, then the trickling sound of urine splattering against the hull. She held her breath. The pants re-zipped. The footsteps moved off.

Her shoulders settled as she finally took a deep breath, but at that moment the man's retreating footsteps stopped. She felt the hair-tingling suspense of his detection. He smelled her. He was sniffing the air. She envisioned him: his chin lifted, nostrils flared. His feet swiveled and he returned. A shadow loomed above her; contours of the face, backlit by the moonlight, were obscured by the murkiness of the night. He peered in, drunkenly angling his head. He whispered something to *Dios* and then fired off into spits of dialogue. His voice was slurred by his intoxication and at the same time freshly curious.

She sat up and slithered back farther into a shadow.

Think of something. A plan. Do something! Make a move!

She could make a run for it, but where was she going to go? She had no idea where she was exactly. The man fumbled in the bottom of the boat, laughing, repeating a man's name.

"Jorge . . . blanca . . . Jorge . . . bueno . . . Jorge . . . mierda."

Her Spanish was minimal. She caught only pieces of what he was saying.

Jorge—white—Jorge—good—Jorge—shit.

His hand found something and he tugged, falling backwards. Surely she could take this guy. He was wasted. Yet the man regained control, chortling at his own clumsiness. He sang, his breath reeking, often adding drunken woo-woo-woos into his garbled lyrics. Harmless. She started to make her way out of the boat.

Ouch! Wait—what was *that*? He snatched her arm and wrapped the rope twice quickly around her wrists. She heard the flick of something metal. The moonlight caught the shine; her eyes widened at the blade. The drunk guffawed at her expression before sawing off the excess end of rope. Okay, so he wasn't going to cut her into pieces, but why the prisoner treatment? What had she ever done to this guy?

His hands were agile even in his intoxication. It was clear he'd spent a lifetime filleting fish, tying nimble-fingered knots to secure lures. He pulled her from the boat with the strength of a man who lifted weighted nets for a living. Once she was on her feet, he feasted on her nudity in the moonlight. She swallowed, disgusted, rage tightening in her chest. Her eyes cut to slits. He tightened the grip on her upper arm and tugged.

In the distance, she saw the silhouettes of huts on a hill, only one hut glowing. They both stumbled in the darkness on the sandy path. It was hard to keep her balance with her hands bound and no other lights except the moon. She glanced around. Was there anyone besides this guy to hear her if she screamed? That's when she noticed there were no power lines. She shuddered at the thought of the inside of the hut where he was taking her.

They reached the crest of the path, and a desert breeze swept around them, her matted hair unrelenting even in the warm gust. The boundless ocean shimmered out to the horizon in one direction. In the opposite, hills stained the color of an eggplant by the night sky rose just high enough to present a looming fortress.

"Jorge!" the drunk man suddenly shouted. They were approaching the front of the lighted hut.

Movement stirred inside, but the door remained closed. The drunk, still grasping her arm, repeated his shouts like a child throwing a tantrum.

"Jorge-Jorge-Jorge-Jorge!"

Geez. The clamor in her ears. *The breath.*

The door opened. A man stood holding a lantern. The drunk ceased his shouting. This must be Jorge: a salted, slate scruff for a beard, skinny in that old-man sort of way, barefoot and shirtless. The sternum of his chest protruded like a dinosaur bird. He had the unmistakable profile of the man who'd found her on the beach.

Jorge barked back at the drunk until his eyes adjusted and he saw her, standing there in all her naked glory. He grew silent for a moment, then spit in the dust. He shouted, but she couldn't understand him.

"*Yell-yell-yell*, Esteban! *Shout-shout-shout*, Esteban!" was all she heard.

She should've paid more attention in high school Spanish.

Esteban bellowed back. He pointed behind him to the beach. Jorge lowered the lantern to show his leg, red and dreadfully swollen. Stingray.

Esteban cackled at the injury but ceased his interrogation. She felt a tug and was jerked into the hut. She glanced around the tiny room. A wooden chair with a broken arm. A mattress on wooden pallets. A battered pot hissing above a wood-fired stove top. Esteban rummaged through the paltry shelves. He uncorked a bottle with his teeth, drank heavily, and wiped his mouth with his sleeve.

Should she make a run for it? Surely she could outrun these two. One guy was drunk and the other was injured.

Jorge limped over and set a blanket around her shoulders. A stench bombarded her nostrils—unwashed skin and smoke, fish scales and seawater—but she wrapped the cover close.

Jorge's eyes cut to Esteban. He hobbled across the room and took two musty glasses off a shelf. Snatching the bottle from Esteban's hands, Jorge filled the small glasses and handed one to Esteban. Esteban slammed the shot back and leaned against the wall. Throwing back the amber liquid in his own glass, the old man exhaled.

Jorge looked at her and grunted. His sinewy arm extended to offer her a shot.

She hesitated, considering. No doubt she could use a shot of something right now, but she glanced at the filthy glass and declined. Jorge poured both men another. After the fourth shot, Esteban slid down the wall; his body fell limp and teetered to one side in a dusty splash on the earthen floor.

Jorge hobbled to the pot on the stove. As he stoked the coals with his breath, he stole glances in her direction. The whites of his bulging eyes gleamed each time the embers flared.

The sounds of the nearby ocean reminded her of her best option. She just had to get rid of the ropes binding her wrists.

She presented her arms to the old man. "Cut," she said definitively.

She nodded to her wrists again. She had to get her wrists untied. "Por favor," she added.

The old man reached for a knife above the stove. He sawed at the rope, mumbling in anger, presumably at the way this night was unfolding. When the rope was sawed to only a thin strip, he set the blade aside and tugged with opposing fists. The remaining rope popped. She circled her freed wrists. The two looked at each other, puzzled.

Still holding the rope, Jorge dropped his hands and backed away. She moved hastily, sloughing the blanket from her shoulders and circumventing the room to slip out of the hut. The old man limped behind her, futilely calling after her. She scuttled through a maze of dry brush, praying she didn't discover a cactus patch with bare feet. Just in time, the moon passed from behind a cloud, illuminating the steep trail down to the beach, like a thin dark scar on the hill.

3

SHE BENT OVER AND RESTED BOTH HANDS ON HER KNEES, her chest heaving. She listened, but heard nothing—the old man hadn't followed her. Her relief lasted only a moment.

There was no electricity in the village, no phones, no radios. The old man had used lanterns to light his house, wood to fuel his stove. The nearest city could be miles away. Waiting until morning was a risk. Escaping across miles of unforgiving desert was not an option.

Her heart pounded in her chest. Waves rumbled from rolls of mercury into crashing, white tantrums. On the beach, there was a scattering of *pangas* with their motors lifted out of the sand, fueled and ready for the fishermen to leave at dawn. The tide was too low now, but she could wait, hide in the rocks. No—moving a boat with a motor and full tank of fuel by herself was impossible. She wasn't even sure she could pull-start the motor if she got the boat in the water. Plus, stealing a boat would certainly rouse the men from the huts. She had to be more realistic.

She laughed. Was swimming away realistic?

"This is crazy," she whispered. But she knew there was no other way.

She took a deep breath, charged into the foaming surf, and dove beneath a curling breaker. She resurfaced, the icy water making her gasp.

"Hard part's over," she said, her voice stilted by the cold. Her foot brushed something slimy, and she lurched and squealed. She closed her eyes.

"Still a good plan, Ishmael. You can do this."

She paddled with her arms and frog-kicked her feet to get beyond the breaking waves. The reflection of the moon on the water was dimpled and golden, like the rind of a lemon. She swam toward the horizon, ignoring the doubts flooding her mind and her fearful imaginings of what was out there swimming with her. Using only her arms to propel her, she let her feet drag behind. Wasn't that how it happened before? She could barely remember. The past few days—or was it weeks?—were a blur of bizarre memories.

She knew she could swim farther and faster if only her body could somehow return to that other form. That . . . aquatic form.

The last vivid recollection she had of her mother flashed through her mind.

Anna had come into the kitchen, tears still wet on her face, and kissed Ishmael on the forehead.

"Why don't you go for a swim, Mommy?" Ishmael had asked.

Life got Ishmael's mother down at times, but in the water, Anna had a way of reviving herself. Ishmael had spent a great deal of her childhood playing on the shore while her mother swam off in the distance. But that day long ago, when Ishmael looked up from her sandcastle, there was nothing but endless water. A lifeguard showed up. Then a man on a four-wheeler. Boats. A helicopter. Cops stopped by daily for weeks. Reporters called. Flowers were delivered. Sympathy cards. Casseroles.

The incident was reported as "an accident." No way it was suicide, her father had said. Wiping tears from his daughter's face while he tucked the covers around her, he'd told Ishmael that her mother had swam off into the sunset as a mermaid.

A mermaid.

Wasn't that just something a dad told his daughter to take away the sting of a mother's death? She'd never *really* thought he was telling the truth, had she?

Until now.

She felt the twisting sensation in her legs. It hurt, but she welcomed the discomfort. She was scared, but she couldn't deny that she was also relieved. Relieved and curious. This time she was more alert.

The skin below her navel and down her legs suddenly felt padded, like she'd been zipped tightly into a warm sleeping bag. The bulk was burdensome, but she sensed that it made her more buoyant. Her feet fanned out; the webbing stretched like putty, connecting the gaps between each toe. She felt as if she were wearing thick stockings and someone was carefully pulling them off, somehow lengthening her flesh with each tug.

With her two legs joined, she gained strength from her lower half; she felt more power and control. What had been her feet and toes was now one massive flipper. It amazed her how easy it was for her to maneuver this new extension of her body, how instinctual.

She reached down with her hands and felt the thick skin beneath her belly button. She patted this new skin down her body until she reached what had been her ankles. There were no scales. She was not a fish. She was a woman with a tail for legs and a fluke for feet.

"Whoa. Wow. It *worked*."

Kicking her tail, she propelled herself out of the water and into the air so that she lifted and arched. She felt a brief exhilaration but lost control, unsure of how to handle this new body hurtling through the air. She flopped back into the ocean with a clumsy splash. Choking, she brushed clumps of hair from her face.

"Okay, so I'm not ready for *that* move yet."

She flexed her abdominal muscles and lifted her lower half so her tail was visible at the surface.

"I don't believe this. This is insane."

She dropped her tail back down and realized that she could easily move her fluke beneath her so that she hovered like a hummingbird in the water. She was able to steer herself up and down with mere flicks of this new appendage. She trailed her hands across the surface and laughed at the phosphorescence in the water, giddy with astonishment.

"Okay, Ishmael. Now what?"

She glanced around, hoping for some sort of answer or guidance. Finally, she tilted her head back and looked up to the masculine face on the lunar surface above her.

She couldn't go back to Nicholas. He said he loved her—enough to put a gigantic diamond on her finger—but did he love her enough to take her seriously? He didn't exactly think outside the box. He would never believe this.

But Allen might.

Bastard, she said, slapping the water. She hadn't spoken to Allen in years.

She looked down at her left hand. The engagement ring was gone. She felt both guilt and exhilaration.

She tipped her head back with a sigh and admired the comfort her tail gave her as she hovered effortlessly in the water. With a strong kick, she dove underwater, and her tail breached the surface gracefully. She kept her arms extended out before her to help with balance. She felt the water stream past her and sensed her wake trailing behind her like a long, billowing gown. Her breath was heavy when she reached the surface. Water dripped from her face, causing her to blink. She puffed the droplets off her lips with heavy exhales, but she was feeling more confident in her ability to negotiate this new form.

She dove again, and this time she kept her arms at her sides and used only her tail to propel her forward. She was wobbly at first, but quickly she found a way to relax her arms and balance in the water without twisting or rolling to one side. She could feel strength all the way down her spine, her body surging forward with the movement initiated by her tail.

Not prepared for this kind of exertion, she surfaced often for air. Adrenaline pounded through her veins and drove her forward. She wasn't sure exactly where she was, but she suspected she was still in Baja and home was to the north. She swam fast, checking her position when she surfaced. Her pace was astounding with this tail, possibly even reckless. She paused with heavy breaths, making sure the land was directly to her right. She planned to hug the shore in order to stay the course.

With this speed, she hoped she'd reach the States before sunrise.

4

THE WAVES CARRIED HER TO THE LAND. There was no way she could swim to shore against an opposing pull. She was bone-tired, grateful for the incoming tide. The pebbly sand beneath assured her she'd made it. Resting her head on the soggy pillow of the shore, she blinked her eyes at the familiar lights of the 101. Only one car passed. No one was around at this perfect hidden hour. Night owls were tucked in bed. Joggers' alarm clocks were yet to chime.

She pushed up onto her elbows and inched forward, dragging her fluke behind her, grunting at the task. Just when she thought she was in the clear, the sea rushed in, showing her the little progress she had made. She plopped back onto her face, the sand crunching in her teeth as she rolled onto her back.

Light pollution. There were so many less stars here than there had been in Baja.

Baja. She'd just swum back *from Baja*.

She rolled onto her belly. No one could find her like this.

She spun onto her back again. This was the way to get herself out of the water: she'd roll herself to dry land. A clumsy movement, but at least she could make progress with each flop of her hulking lower half.

After countless turns, she paused, a bit dizzy. Chest heaving. She closed her eyes. A gracious moment of rest. She could've happily slept there.

As her breath slowed, her body dried in the gentle breeze coming off the ocean. Like a heavy blanket pulled away, she felt the thick skin of her lower half returning to normal. When she sensed that she could move her legs separately, she pulled the two apart. An interesting release: like when she was a young girl and her father would bury her in the sand and she would pry herself out of his mold.

She reached down and felt the thick tail skin dissolving, thinning to a slimy egg-white layer. She propped herself up on her elbows. In the dim glimmer from the nearby lights of the parking lot, she watched thicker clumps of skin slough away. The process was disgusting and fascinating. Her toes began to re-form like buds on a limb in spring. She was a wax sculpture remolded. She wiggled her toes, a movement so foreign and yet so easy.

Could she stand? So soon?

She spun onto her belly and pushed up onto all fours, her body aching with exhaustion. Headlights swept a distant hillside road and revved her adrenaline. She put one foot into the sand and pressed her hands to standing. She wobbled a bit, amazed. Like a newborn foal, her strength and balance came quickly.

Once out of the sand, she picked up the pace to a trot, her bare feet tender on the concrete. She hid behind a bush and waited for a lone car to pass. Checking both directions, she darted across the 101 and crouched in a thicket. She paused, holding her breath and listening. Coast was clear. She raced across the train tracks in the direction of the coffee shop.

A metal fire escape to the rear of the shop led up to Allen's apartment. The latch was broken on the window at the top of the staircase. Hopefully Allen hadn't decided to get that fixed.

She looked up at the window: his lights were off. Allen was an early riser, but she had no idea what time it was.

Wait—what the *hell* was she doing? What was she going to say to him? She'd been missing for god-only-knew how many days, she was naked, and she was about to climb through the window of her ex-boyfriend's apartment?

She chewed her nails for a moment and then slammed her hands down by her sides.

No No No. No backing out now. She was here. Nicholas's apartment was miles away, perched on a high cliff in a gated community.

Allen would believe her. Father Allen Wilson? Of course he would—a perfect blend of spiritual and grounded. He would help her figure this out. He'd been a priest for a stint in his earlier life. Listened to confessions, offered prayers. He'd have answers.

Her hand grasped the railing, and the rush of the cold metal encouraged her to take the first step. She climbed the staircase and reached out from the landing at the top. The window slid open.

"*Allen*," she whispered, poking her head inside.

Nothing. She climbed through the window and repeated his name again. Silence. She crept toward the bed on tiptoe and dropped to flat feet. The room was empty and the sheets were tidy. She glanced around, looking for clues, and caught a whiff of incense burning in the corner, the spicy stick only half-spent. Allen must be down in the shop. She hadn't seen any lights on downstairs, but maybe he was in the storeroom, organizing the latest shipment of supplies before the morning rush.

She looked around the all-too-familiar apartment. A few old surfboards were tucked up in the exposed rafters; artwork, shells, postcards, and photographs adorned the walls. A wooden sculpture of the Madonna stood in a corner, the rustic Virgin's palms open to welcome the lost and weary.

She walked across the room and stood by the phone. She had to call Nicholas. He must be a wreck. He would be ecstatic to have her back, to know she was alive.

She reached for the phone, but her hand snatched back.

Her wedding invitation peeked out of a stack on the counter. *Holy shit!* They'd invited Allen?

Granted, Allen was a bit of a community icon. And practically all of southern California had been on the guest list. Who invites that many people to their wedding? Who has that many friends? Certainly not her.

She picked up the phone and held it to her ear. The dial tone whined in the background as she muttered to herself, practicing.

"Hey, babe. It's me . . . I know, but I can explain . . ."

Forget that. She couldn't explain.

"Hey babe, it's me . . . I'm in Cardiff at the coffee shop. . . . Yeah, Allen's coffee shop . . ."

Well, she could forget that too.

The door to the apartment opened. She exhaled, looking across the room, and placed the phone back on the cradle.

5

"ALLEN. HEY." Her voice was scratchy. "I can explain."

He came closer. "Ish—what the—what are you doing here?"

Now in his late forties, he'd aged impressively, a chiseled structure beneath his tan skin. Only a few gray hairs were visible in his sun-drenched, russet hair. He had that weathered surfer look she loved.

"You smell like peanut butter," she said, drawing her hand away from the phone.

"I was—on a walk," he said. He pointed over his shoulder to the door of the apartment as if that explained. "Couldn't sleep."

She gave a weak smile. "PB&J for breakfast. That's still your thing?"

"Ish, what happened to you? I've been so—" He swallowed his words. "Everyone thinks you're dead."

Yeah, ah—about that. Can I have a sip of water before I answer that? I'm parched," she said, stalling.

She moved into the kitchen, too tired to care that she was

unclothed. She took a glass from the cabinet and turned the faucet on. She stood over the sink and chugged the water, exhaling heavily as she set the glass down.

"Where have you been?" he asked. "How—why are you here?"

She was already refilling and gulping greedily. She turned and faced his gaze.

"I know I have a lot of explaining to do," she said. She offered a faint smile. "I'm not sure I understand it all myself. But I couldn't go home. Small park. Nosy neighbors. This was the only other safe place I could think of."

She walked the few steps to the bathroom and retrieved a towel from a hook, wrapping it around her body.

"Can I take a shower?" she asked.

"Whatever you need. . .where are your clothes?"

"I'm not trying to put you in a difficult situation. I really—I just—had nowhere else to go."

"Look, of course I'm glad you're back—you're alive—you're here, but—" His voice pulsed with emotion. "But Ish, you're engaged."

She nodded. "I almost forgot." She looked at him and smiled. He didn't smile back.

"Okay. You got me." She shifted her stance nervously. "I have absolutely no idea what I'm doing."

"Decision's been made for you," he said. "The wedding was canceled."

"Man, how long have I been gone?"

"Seventeen days."

"Someone's been counting."

He puffed a laugh, looking at her in disbelief.

"This is serious, Ish," he said. "Where have you been?"

"What'd they do with all my paintings and clothes and stuff? I had this great canvas I was working on . . ."

"Did you not hear me? Where the hell have you been?"

"I heard you," she said. "Loud and clear. I just don't have an answer yet."

"And since when did you have dreadlocks?" he asked, relaxing a bit. "I wouldn't have thought Nicholas would be into that kind of thing."

The last thing on her mind was her tangled hair and whether Nicholas would approve.

He finally spoke. "They haven't done anything with your stuff. The trailer's still in your dad's name, so they can't really do anything without his permission."

"That takes a load off."

"There've been offers though," he said. "To buy your trailer. That's what I hear, at least. Some guy who lives in that million-dollar trailer park up in Malibu is trying to get his hands on it. Your trailer has a rooftop deck. Makes it worth more."

"Screw that. They can't sell my trailer right out from under me."

"Look, don't freak out," he said. "I heard Nicholas already paid the space rent for the next few months."

She exhaled relief and laughed faintly.

"Of course he did. Good ole Nicholas saves the day," she said.

She looked to Allen and then down at her hands.

"Damn," she said. "I screwed that up, didn't I?"

"What were you doing down there anyways? Why go to Baja in the first place?"

"Nicholas and I had a huge fight."

"Dare I ask?"

"He wanted to use some connection he had in a foreign embassy to find my dad."

"Hmm." Allen's mind seemingly drifted into thoughts of the past. "And that's wrong because . . . ?"

"Any dad who heads down to South America on a surf trip and doesn't call his daughter for *nine years* is not worth the search."

"So you just decided to disappear yourself?"

"*No*. I went to Baja—*if you must know*—because I'd tracked down the priest that married my parents. I was hoping to find some information about my mom."

He nodded slowly, his gaze meeting hers. He understood her past and what this meant to her.

"Just so you know, Nicholas didn't want me to go alone to Baja either," she said. "He was super busy because it was so close to the . . ." Her voice trailed off briefly. "Anyways, he'd already taken a bunch of time off."

"You can say it. Wedding. I got an invitation."

She exhaled heavily. "Yeah. I should have known this would be too weird."

"No. Look. Nicholas wanted you to invite your dad to the wedding, didn't he?" He shrugged. "That's noble enough."

She eased onto a nearby stool, readjusting her towel, grateful to give her tired legs a rest.

"Nicholas was frustrated that I wanted to research my long-lost mom rather than track down my dad. He told me I had my priorities all mixed up. And maybe I do. *Shoot*. Anyway. He told me he'd take me down there on the yacht after we got married. Make a vacation out of it. Said I wouldn't have to lift a finger."

He looked at her for a moment. "Knowing you, I'm sure that pissed you off," he said. "His offer to pamper you."

She swallowed, not wanting to admit how well he knew her.

"You didn't screw anything up, Ish. You were in a car accident. It wasn't your fault." His eyebrows lifted. "You *were* in a car accident, right?"

"I meant I screwed up by coming *here*—to you."

She looked at him. His jaw was clenched.

"That came out wrong," she said. She pulled at a loose thread on the towel, letting the air clear. "So, you've already brought him up. Spill the beans. What do you know? Where is he?"

"Who?"

"My dad."

Allen walked across the room.

"I know as much as you do," he said, crossing his arms over his chest as he looked out the window. He stood in the one spot in the apartment that afforded an ocean view. She knew the sight of the waves in the early grey light soothed him. "Your dad's probably still in South America somewhere. After your accident, I reached out to a few ex-pat buddies of mine down there. Nobody's seen him in years."

"So he doesn't even know about the accident?"

"Unless he reads the American papers online."

"Typical. Dad's MIA."

"Hate to mention it, but so are you." He crossed the room and started fumbling in the kitchen. "There are more clean towels in the—well, you know where the towels are."

"If this is too much, I can—"

She stood again and winced at the strain. Everything seemed to ache.

"No. It's fine," he said. "I'm fine. I'll give you some privacy. I'll go help Eleanor downstairs." He took his hooded sweatshirt off a hook and pulled it on over his head. "I just hope I don't go downstairs and come back to find that this was only a dream. You're really here, aren't you?"

"Barely," she said. "But this is me. More than I know what to do with."

"What's that supposed to mean?"

"It means I need some time to figure all this out. And I'd appreciate if you —"

"I have no intentions of saying anything to anyone, Ish. I can wait on the answers. As long as—"

He caught himself.

"As long as I only share my secrets with you," she said.

She knew from the look on his face that she was spot on. She felt the wooly beast of resentment waking from its hibernation in her chest.

"You just love secrets, don't you?" she asked.

She couldn't believe she'd said it. Immediately she wanted to take it back. She'd come here because she trusted him, not to argue. She'd forgiven him. Why couldn't she admit that?

"It was *one* night, Ish. I've said I'm sorry a hundred times. You know if I could take it back I would. It broke my heart when you left me."

"And you don't think you broke mine?"

She'd never told him that.

He looked at her. "You're not wearing your ring."

She bit her lip, not able to make eye contact. "I lost it in the wreck."

"Of course."

"Just give me some more time," she said. "I'll sort this out."

"You know I will. I'll give you anything I can. But the facts don't add up, Ish. You couldn't possibly have survived that." He stared at her, scanning her face for an explanation. "I have a million questions."

In her silence, he turned to go but then paused with his hand on the doorknob.

"I don't want to leave this room," he said.

Then don't, she was tempted to say, but she remained silent.

"That shirt of mine you used to always wear is still in the bottom drawer," he said. "I still have a pair of your jeans too. And don't give me any crap about that being creepy. It's not like I take them out and smell them or anything."

He looked at her before opening the door. She loved his brown eyes.

"Listen, I guess I should just come out and say it. I—well— thank you. For coming here. For trusting me. For giving me a second chance."

"Allen, it's not like I'm—"

He held up a hand to shush her. "Just—thank you. Let's leave it at that. I shouldn't have added the second part."

A dimpled grin broke through on his serious face, and she couldn't resist smiling back.

"I'll be here when you get back," she said.

"Just take a bath," he urged. "Not a shower. You look whipped. I'm worried about you standing in the steam and all."

She wasn't sure whether she liked him babying her. There was no denying she liked the attention, but Allen was almost two decades older. He could get overbearing, paternal. But then, there was that smile again. *Damn.* Before she could stop, another grin washed over her face in response. She walked across the room, pursing her lips to contain it.

"Get out of here. Let me shower," she said, pressing a hand into his chest.

He covered her hand with his and held it there. She felt the hardness of his sternum, the definition of his muscles, the sweetness of those maple syrup eyes.

"No shower," he said. "*Bath.*"

"Got it. No shower."

She nodded and pushed him out the door. She wasn't quite ready to offer an explanation if the bathtub caused her to change back into a mermaid again.

6

THE LAST OF THE WATER DRAINED completely from the tub with one final gurgle as she wrapped a towel around her dripping body, her legs still intact. Bending over the sink, she slurped water out of her cupped palm and then caught a glimpse of her profile in the mirror. She used her hand to wipe away the condensation.

Wow.

She hadn't looked in a mirror in over a week. It wasn't so much her appearance—sure, her hair was a complete wreck—but more, it was that she felt like she was seeing herself for the first time. She stared at the woman before her, feeling her feet on the cold tile floor and thinking of the tail she had seen in their place.

She looked again at herself in the mirror and then opened a drawer and pulled out a pair of scissors. The dreads had to go. Looping her fingers through the handles, she snipped the first large mat of hair. She needed a clean slate. As each clump of hair fell to the floor, she felt lighter. Tangles gone, she plugged in Allen's electric clippers and traced the first stripe across her head from front to back.

"Like cutting the grass," she said as the first row of stubble appeared.

She finished the rest of the tracks and then gazed at herself, checking out the woman she hardly recognized in the mirror.

"Just like that," she said, turning her head to view from all angles.

She was blowing hairs off the clippers when the bathroom door swung open. A high-heeled redhead stood in the doorway.

"Well, *that's* certainly got my attention," the woman said.

The redhead wore a skin-tight skirt that complemented her every curve. Her blouse was the flashy bright coral of a hibiscus flower.

"What in the name of heaven is she doing here?" the redhead asked Allen.

Allen looked at Ishmael standing in his bathroom in only a towel and grinned.

"Ish—what happened to your hair?" he asked.

"Got rid of it."

"I like it," he said.

"You could've *at least* told me you had company when I called this morning," the redhead said. "Dammit-all-straight-to-hell. This pisses me off! Can't you keep that thing in your pants?"

Even in her anger, her voice had the honey-sweet drawl of a southern accent.

"Shhh!" Allen whispered. "Keep your voice down. *Please.* We've got customers right below us."

The redhead inhaled quickly. "Don't you *shush* me!"

"It's not what you think," Allen defended. "I haven't been keeping anything from you. She just showed up here this morning."

Ishmael stepped out of the bathroom, nodding in acknowledgement.

"Hey. I remember you," Ishmael said. "I ran your husband's

charter business after Allen cheated on me and I quit the coffee shop."

Allen threw his arms up in the air. "It was *one night!*"

Ishmael tightened the towel around her.

"I really liked working for Captain Harry," she said. "Salty as they come. How is he?"

"Oh, he's doing fabulous. Just added another boat to the fleet, darling. And like all of us, he thinks you're *dead*. Now you want to tell me what the hell you're doing here?"

"Your name's Diane, right? Wait—" Ishmael turned to Allen. "A *married* woman? I wouldn't have thought you'd take it this far."

"Ish, I didn't—she's not—*we're* not—listen, this is crazy. Diane and I are just friends. I got her to—"

"I'm listening," Ishmael said.

"Me too," Diane said. "This ought to be good."

"Ish, you're being paranoid," Allen said. "We're not sleeping together. I wouldn't lie to you."

Ishmael crossed her arms.

Diane chimed in. "Hon, trust me. I want nothing to do with those scrawny legs. Now let's all get back to the subject of you and what you're doing here."

"Scrawny legs!" Allen bellowed as he peered down incredulously.

"Yes, darling," Diane said, giving her attention briefly to Allen. "You've got a nice back. But your legs are not your forte."

She turned back to Ishmael with a grin. "I like a man with some girth."

Diane primped her hair, brushing thick curls from her neck with the flip of a wrist. Her fingernails were the cherry red shine of a sports car.

"I like my legs," Allen said. "Beatrice likes my legs. I always catch her checking them out."

"Hold up. I didn't mean to get us side-tracked," Diane said.

"Beatrice?" Ishmael said. "No way! Non-fat-half-caff-soy-latte Beatrice? She's still around? Wow. That means she's been unsuccessfully trying to sleep with you for over a decade."

"Really? Beatrice?" Allen suddenly grew pensive as Ishmael rolled her eyes and stomped off to the dresser.

"Hmm. A little jealousy. I *like* it." Diane moved into the kitchen. "Like watching a movie. I think I need some refreshments to go with this drama."

"Look, Ish. The fact is, we're business partners now—Diane and me," Allen said. "I got in a little too deep with my side business a few years back, and instead of losing the coffee shop, Diane stepped in and bought a hefty chunk of the joint."

"No pun intended on *the joint* part," Diane said, peering into the fridge. Ishmael looked up from the drawer she was searching through.

"Ah. Yes. Your *drug-smuggling* side business," Ishmael said. "Why, Allen! I'm so surprised those marijuana dealings didn't work out for you."

"We're You Java Wonder, LLC now," he explained. "I don't own the shop outright anymore."

Ishmael found the shirt she was looking for. "I can't believe she let you keep that *ridiculous* name," she said as she slid the shirt over her head.

"You gotta wonder, right?" Diane said from the kitchen.

"Diane handles the business stuff and nobody even knows she's involved," he said. "We're partners. *Business* partners. That's it."

Ishmael slid the jeans on, the towel still wrapped around her waist.

"I don't get it," she said, zipping and buttoning. "Your jackass self swore up and down you'd *never* take on a partner. I asked once if I could buy into the shop and you told me 'no'."

"Yes, well—that was before he got in over his head," Diane said. She was adding hot sauce to a glass of tomato juice. "Speaking of getting in over your head, tell me again what *you're* doing here, sugar lump?"

Allen was suddenly busy in the kitchen.

"What the hell have you two been up to?" Diane demanded, cutting her eyes at Allen. "Have you been hiding her up here this whole time?"

"Of course not!" Allen's brow furrowed with intensity. He ran his hands through his hair.

"Well, who the hell was in that truck that went off the cliff?" Diane slammed the hot sauce jar down and crossed her arms over her chest.

"I was," Ishmael said from across the room.

Allen leaned resignedly against the counter.

"Diane's a walking lie detector, Ish. You might as well just tell her. She'll get it out of you one way or another."

"Okay. So—my truck went off a cliff. And then—well, then I was rescued by this—shoot, I don't know how to explain this."

"Rescued? How'd you even survive?" Diane asked. "Woo-wee." She exhaled at the spiciness after a sip from her glass. "I'm putting my money on a bet that your rich fiancé orchestrated some sort of switch-a-roo and it wasn't really you in that truck that went off the cliff. Maybe a mannequin or something. Hmm. I'm trying to think. This some sort of insurance scam or something? You can tell me. I'm good and tight with secrets."

She slid her eyes from Allen to Ishmael, assessing the situation.

"Darling, I'm rather surprised at the way you're handling this. I'm not sure what possesses a woman to shave her head and hide out in her ex-boyfriend's apartment, but it's got to be something out of the ordinary. You got something chasing your tail, sugar?"

Ishmael exhaled heavily. "Something like that."

Ishmael moved past Diane and into the kitchen. She opened a cabinet by the fridge and pulled out an opened bottle of wine, yanking the cork out with her back teeth.

"Well, somebody knows just where Father Allen hides his communion wine," Diane said.

Allen glanced down at his watch. "It's barely morning, Ish."

Ishmael glared at him. "You got anything stronger?"

She opened another cabinet and pulled out a cup decorated with turtles and dolphins frolicking in the ocean. The sea creatures and waves were painted in a handsome palette arrayed within an Aztec pattern, giving the childish subject matter a striking motif.

"Dude, this is my mug. I *love* this mug. Painted this in the tenth grade. I can't believe I left this here."

Diane started rummaging through her purse. She passed a silver flask to Ishmael.

"Sweetie, I'll be honest. You smell bad."

Ishmael put the mug down and unscrewed the top.

"I do? Still?" She chased her questions with a hefty swig and then breathed out the fumes. "I just took a bath."

"You smell like seaweed or something," Diane answered, wrinkling her nose. "You smell like my husband when he comes home from work. It's rugged and sexy on him, but on you—sugar, I would recommend a bit more scrubbing next time. Scented bath salts. A loofah or something."

Ishmael took another sip and passed the flask back to Diane.

"Listen, hon, I have no clue what or why or how you got here, but I feel it's my duty as a woman to urge you to call Nicholas. He at least deserves to know you're alive."

"Not yet." Ishmael poured wine into the mug she had found. "I need more time to think things through."

"But you're just creating a bigger mess with every moment you avoid this. You're snowballing here, darling."

Ishmael was running out of excuses. She walked over to the couch and sat down, sipping her wine.

"I'm in a different place," she said.

"Ain't that the truth. You look like you're in the military," Diane said.

"I think she looks pretty hot," Allen said from the kitchen. "Seriously. Very Sinead O'Connor. Nothing compares to you, Ish."

Diane rolled her eyes.

"If that doesn't make you want to go running back to your fiancé, I don't know what will." Diane looked more intently at Ishmael. "You sure you know what you're doing here, darling? You're positive?"

"Positive. Nicholas wouldn't understand."

Diane tossed up her hands. "No use beating a dead horse. I can see you don't love him." Diane joined Ishmael on the couch. "And—well, I probably shouldn't say this because I'm not really sure what you're up to, darling, but—you've got my vote." Diane patted Ishmael's leg once and then added, "I've never been a huge fan of those Santorinis." She pouted. "Broke my little ole Captain Harry's heart when he found out you were marrying into that family. Harry thought you better suited for a man's man, if you know what I mean." Diane winked at Ishmael. "Less hair gel. More pickup truck."

Ishmael leaned back against the pillows on the couch. "Nicholas doesn't use hair gel."

Diane dismissively patted Ishmael on the thigh.

"So, darling, let's get back to the real question of what in the hell you're doing here? *Alive?*"

7

DIANE'S PHONE ERUPTED FROM HER PURSE with a flamboyant southern rock ringtone. She peered at the caller id. "Damn-*nation!* I've got to take this," she said, ducking out of the room onto the landing at the top of the stairs.

"Hello?" Her voice trilled with professional politeness. "Oh, yes, yes. This is she. Oh, *I know*. We had the reservation on the books, but . . ."

Ishmael slid onto a barstool in the kitchen.

"Hey—do you remember the first time you met my dad?" she asked.

"Ish, I really don't—" He caught the look on her face. "Of course. I'd just moved here."

"You were the first person to make him smile since Mom was gone."

"Your dad and I were the dawn patrol duo. Surfed together every morning."

He smiled at the memory as he flipped strips of bacon in the skillet with metal tongs. She set her mug down on the counter, her fingers still tucked into the familiar handle. Being back in this apartment, with Allen cooking for her, made emotions swirl in her chest.

"You were my first real crush," she said. She only slightly regretted admitting this.

"Oh, yeah?" he asked, the dimple reappearing. "The others weren't real?"

"There was only one before you. And I was just a kid."

She paused a moment too long, staring at him.

"You were older, and that was cool when I was young," she said. "Then I found out you'd been a priest. Made you a good guy. And the fact that you'd *left* the priesthood, well, that made you kind of a bad guy. It was the perfect balance."

She swirled the liquid in her mug.

"But what you did with my dad. That sealed the deal."

He was pensive for a moment, staring down at the frying pan.

"Your dad had a hard time letting go of your mom," he said. "He really loved her."

He cracked eggs into a bowl and started whisking them.

"That's why I'm here." She leaned in. "Allen, I think my mom might still be alive."

He paused briefly, his expression ambiguous, and then went back to whisking eggs.

"I never told you this—I never told anybody this—but after my mom's disappearance, my dad told me she wasn't dead."

He looked up at her.

"He told me my mom swam off into the sunset."

He half-laughed.

"When I was a priest, that's what I liked to call a *tender* lie," he said. "You were young. Your dad was doing the best he could."

She took a deep breath.

"Yeah, well, he told me she swam away because she was a mermaid."

The toaster oven dinged. The tops of browned bread slices popped up.

"And what, you *believed* him?" he asked.

"I was six years old."

Allen dropped the spatula and put both hands on Ishmael's shoulders, looking her in the eyes.

"Ish, what are you hiding?" he asked. "Did something happen to you in the accident? Did you hit your head or something?" He shifted so he could keep her gaze as she averted her eyes. "We can work this out. There's no need to be scared."

"I'm not hiding anything!" she said. "I'm trying to tell you that—well—I'm—"

She slid off the barstool and moved away.

"You can tell me anything," he said. Genuine sincerity glistened in his chestnut eyes. "Anything. Whatever it is, I'll help you through this. Just tell me exactly what happened."

"Okay. Well. I'm a mermaid," she said. She exhaled triumphantly. "There. I said it."

He raised his eyebrows wordlessly. Perhaps she was just being overly optimistic, but his face didn't give the impression that he thought she was totally crazy. Now that the first die was cast, she felt emboldened.

"That's how I survived the accident. Someone—or *something*—pulled me from the wreckage. I don't really remember much, but . . ."

He looked intensely at her.

"You don't believe me, do you?" she asked.

"Just—tell me more," he said. "How do you know this? What makes you think that you're a . . . mermaid?"

"Well, I—I was pulled from my truck underwater by some—thing. Whatever it was, it saved me. And it was fast. It towed me away from my sinking truck and brought me to the surface to breathe when I needed to and it—it had a tail."

"None of this makes you a mermaid, Ish." He glared at her. "How'd you get back here?"

"Well, I didn't have any clothes on and I was in this boat. I woke up, and there were all these stars. This drunk dude showed up and he took me to some other dude's hut and that guy—"

"I'm not sure I'm following. Some drunk dude found you? Naked? In a boat?"

"Yeah, but I got away. And I ran for the ocean and dove in and then my legs became this tail—I'm not kidding—and it was so powerful and I felt so strong and I knew I could swim back to the States—"

"A tail, huh?"

Okay, now he was looking at her like she was crazy.

"So you're saying a mermaid rescued you after your truck went off a cliff. But then the mermaid left you in some drunk guy's boat and so you grew your own mermaid tail and swam back here from Baja?"

She didn't move. She didn't know what to say. The story did sound ridiculous.

"You've been gone half a month. You couldn't have been in the bottom of the boat for two weeks. You look fed. How'd you eat? What'd you eat?"

"Fish wrapped in—I guess it was like kelp or something. It was tough."

"The kelp or the fish?"

"Both."

"Was it cooked?"

"Nope."

"So, sushi. You just ate it with your fingers?"

"Kinda. Not really. I mean, yes, with the fingers. But no soy sauce. No ginger or wasabi or anything. Definitely no sake."

"There's more to sushi than the accoutrements."

"I'm not joking, Allen."

"Neither am I."

She'd hoped the truth would set her free. Now, she just felt like a fool.

Allen grew quiet, staring at her. He moved back into the kitchen and started scrambling the eggs in the frying pan.

"I know this all sounds insane," she said. "And impossible. I don't know how it happened." She glanced over toward the landing; the door was barely cracked, and she could hear Diane still gabbing away on the phone. She leaned in closer and lowered her voice. "I had a tail. That's how I got here, Allen. And that's how I survived. I'm not making this up."

Ishmael moved into the kitchen and started opening cabinets.

"We're about to eat," Allen said. "If you could just wait a—"

She cracked open a bag of chips and stuffed a wad in her mouth, grimacing as she read the label on the front.

"Seriously? Who buys salt-free tortilla chips?" she asked.

"Men who let the love of their life slip away and eat crap food for decades, then finally decide to change their ways."

"I was the love of your life?" she asked.

"Yes. And you probably still are." He softened his voice. "But I can't say I believe you. And I think you should see a doctor.

I'm scared you hit your head."

"But what if what my dad told me is actually true? Maybe she did just swim away," Ishmael said, stuffing another handful of chips in her mouth. "Maybe she's out there somewhere."

"I'm going to have the most delicious food on the table in about two minutes. I can't believe you're still eating those."

"Now that I've seen my own body change . . ." Her voice trailed off. Her eyes glazed over, focused on the past. "I don't know, Allen. She's *my mom*. I've always wanted to know the truth of what happened to her. I've always wanted answers. I have this whole separate dimension of my life, deep inside, that completely revolves around her."

She looked over at him.

"People talk about having a hole in your heart when someone is missing from your life, but I don't have a hole: I have questions. Millions of them. I want to know if my mom was an artist like me. I want to know what her favorite color was. I want to know if I have her eyes. I mean, did I make that up—or were her eyes really the exact same color as mine?"

Allen speared the food onto plates.

"A mermaid," he finally said, slicing an avocado and adding garnishes to each plate.

"Yeah. A mermaid. As in, a woman with a tail." She beamed. "It's amazing, right?"

"Just give me a chance to warm up to all this."

Ishmael was distracted by Diane's open purse on the counter: a glass container caught her eye and she pulled it out, unscrewed the cap, and smelled the contents.

"Hey—chick with a tail—you think it's cool to just go through someone's purse like that?"

"You don't believe me at all, do you?" She sprinkled the contents from the container into the bag of chips. "You really think I need to see a doctor?"

"Yes, I do. Because, I actually do believe you. At least, I believe that *you* believe that you're half-fish. And so I think you should see a doctor. And before that, despite what Diane says about me—and despite the fact that Nicholas only drinks Starbucks coffee—I want you to call Nicholas."

"How do you know Nicholas only drinks Starbucks?" she asked.

He took a deep breath, ignoring her question. "Ish, if it were me—if I were the one marrying you—let's just say he deserves to know you're alive."

"I'm impressed."

"Yeah, well, I've matured a bit over the years since we split up."

"No. I'm impressed with this *spice*."

Whatever she had found in Diane's purse was the perfect blend; she savored each bite.

"This is far too complicated for me to handle alone," he said. "You have to call the guy."

She spoke with her mouth full. "I'm going to pretend for a little bit longer that you didn't just say all that and that you're still on my team."

"I am on your team. There's this doctor guy that comes in for coffee all the time. I'm not sure what kind of doctor he is, but I could ask him to—" His nose crinkled. "Man, what's that *smell*?"

She looked around, smelled the bag in her hands.

"What smell?" she said, stuffing more chips into her mouth.

"That smell that smells like the bottom of a fishing boat."

Allen reached in Diane's purse and pulled out the small jar of spices. He opened the lid.

"Whoa—*wow*—yes, that's the smell," he said, pulling his nose quickly away and sealing the jar. "What is that stuff?"

"No idea," she said. "It's probably like nutritional yeast or something."

"Smells like fish food."

She shrugged. "Tastes good."

"*Looks* like fish food."

"Well, that's just, like, your opinion, *man*," she said. She smirked and stuffed another bite in her mouth, watching him, knowing she was pressing his buttons.

"That's not fair. You can't quote *The Big Lebowski* at a time like this."

"A time like what?" she asked. She chewed the last of her mouthful and then swallowed. She smelled the bag again, knowing her blasé attitude would arouse his annoyance. "You know, I really don't think this stuff smells bad."

He started to speak, but then stopped himself, instead forcing a smile. She could see him formulating his argument, choosing his words carefully. He reached out his hands and stopped her from taking another bite.

"Look, Ish, when your dad told you that your mother swam off into the sunset and you believed him—well, it's sweet. But I'm not sure that means your mom—"

She pulled her arms away. "Sweet?"

"Yes. Extremely. But don't you think you're being a bit childish? You've got to understand that—"

"No, YOU understand!" she said. "What the—how can you not trust me? Of all people, I thought *you* would believe me!"

He glanced around for an explanation. "What just happened here?"

"You certainly smoked enough pot and licked enough LSD in your day to expand that mind of yours! I thought you actually might be the one person open to a new possibility! And you were a priest for goodness' sake! I'm *confessing*! Just believe me!"

"Please keep your voice down."

"Screw you! I will not keep my voice down! You believe in immaculate conception but you won't believe that my mom might be a mermaid?"

"I'm not a priest anymore. Listen, I'm not trying to make you mad. I'm trying to be your friend."

"My friend? This is *friends*?" She pointed to the two of them.

"Ish, you know you've always been one to mix fantasy and truth."

She was silent, boiling.

"You blend them together—that's what makes you so creative. That's what makes you such an amazing painter."

"I'm not painting. This is real. It's happening."

She waited for him to say something. Anything.

"What?" she asked in his silence. "*El Padre's* caught off guard because he's so at one with the ocean and yet he's never seen a mermaid out in the line-up?"

She knew she'd really pissed him off now. He hated it when she made fun of his nickname.

"Fine." He stared at her. "You're welcome to prove it to me."

She pretended to be unruffled. "Fine. I'm not exactly sure how, but—"

"Ishmael Morgan, if there is any truth to what you're saying, then I'm going to have to see it with my own eyes."

Diane snapped her phone shut in the doorway.

"Truth to what?"

She sashayed into the kitchen and started directing Allen.

"Not too much, darling," Diane said, pointing toward the plates. "I've got to keep this girlish figure."

Diane snagged a slice of bacon and took a bite as she looked furtively over at Ishmael.

"Truth to what?" she asked again as she opened the fridge and retrieved the orange juice. "Who wants juice?" she asked, already filling three glasses on the counter.

Diane frowned and held up a hand like she was going to sneeze. "*Damn*! What's that smell?" She eyed the container from her purse on the counter. "*Ho-lee*—sugar-pie, did you put that on your corn chips?"

Diane held the bottle up to Ishmael.

"Darling, that's fish food! You know, for the little critters that swim around in a glass bowl with water in it?" Diane squared both fists on her hips. "I was going to stop by the office and sprinkle some in the aquarium after I left here. Captain Harry makes this stuff himself. That's why there's no label." She shook her head. "*Fish food*, sugar-pie!"

Allen shook his head. "Certainly makes sense with the conversation we were just having."

"Shut up, Allen," Ishmael said.

"Ishmael just told me she's a mermaid."

Diane looked up from her purse and perked her ears.

"Thanks for just blurting that out," Ishmael said. "Makes me sound like a total idiot."

"You darn well might be if you're sprinkling that stuff on your nachos!" Diane said. "I will say that Captain Harry makes him some of the best fish food around. Good, clean stuff. Won't hurt you. Whatever floats your boat." Diane extended the container to Ishmael. "Feel free to put some on your eggs if you want to."

Allen was looking intently at Diane. "Diane. Seriously? Were you listening to what I just said?"

"So she's got a little fantasy of being a sexy woman of the sea." Diane shrugged. "Who doesn't?"

Diane started to set the table.

"My Harry swears up and down that he's seen 'em. I just thought he'd been sucking on that pipe of his for too long." She paused for a moment, her eyes growing narrower, thinking. "But we should probably take you to a doctor, darling. Get you checked out. Just to be sure."

"Agreed." Allen pounded his fist on the counter, triumphant.

Diane was already tucking her napkin in her lap.

"I'm not going to lie," Diane said. "I think this is one of the best mornings I've had in years. Reunited lovers and resurrected mermaids. I'm having one hell of a good start to my day. Totally worth skipping my pedicure appointment." Diane picked up her fork. "Y'all mind if I go ahead and eat before mine gets any colder?"

"So tell us, Ish," Allen said from the kitchen, arms still crossed. "Where did this mermaid take you after it rescued you? Where have you been for the past two weeks?"

"It was some sort of sea cave," Ishmael said, joining Diane at the table.

"A mermaid *rescued* you?" Diane asked. "Damn, I missed a *ton* while I was on the phone. Can we rewind and start back at the beginning?"

"They kept me there and nursed me back to full health after the accident," Ishmael said, swallowing her first bite. She was ravenous. "Geez, this is good. I'd forgotten what a great cook you are, Allen."

"And so were there other things with tails there?" Allen asked as he pulled out a chair.

"Other mermaids, you mean?" Ishmael glanced between Diane and Allen, attempting to read their expressions. She couldn't decide if they believed her or if they were just humoring her to play along. "Yeah, there were. I vaguely remember there being males and females. The dude ones had beards."

"So what did these creatures do all day in their sea cave?" Allen asked.

"You don't have to be rude, Allen," Diane said.

With Diane's support, Ishmael felt less tentative.

"Well, they played. Hunted for food. How many adults do you know that just hunt for food and play all day?" Ishmael put another bite in her mouth. "I mean, what do dolphins do all day?" She chewed and swallowed. "They seemed content to just be, I guess. Just to survive. They seemed happy. They kept feeding me this paste that took away the pain but made me drowsy. So I don't remember a lot of details."

"And you ate it? Some random paste that these sea creatures gave you?" he asked.

"Oh, Allen, stop being such a buzz kill," Diane said.

"And no major injuries after your truck went off the cliff?" he asked. "No problems at all?"

Ishmael paused, chewing. She looked down at her body, shrugged.

"I mean, my whole body is sore, but otherwise, yeah, I feel fine."

"Well then, I guess I've got no choice but to see this for myself," Allen said, shoveling salsa over his eggs. "Diane, does Captain Harry still have that 22-footer of his tied up at the marina?" he asked.

"Sure does," Diane nodded assent.

"How about we all take it out for a little spin?" Allen said. "And after that—Ishmael, I hate to say it, but you're going back to Nicholas. I can't get tangled up in this. I've worked way too hard to get my life back on track since we split up."

"I'm happy to prove myself, Allen. But once I do, I'm not going back to Nicholas."

Allen rubbed the back of his neck and looked at Ishmael, slowly chewing his food.

"I just don't recognize you," he said without breaking his gaze. "I don't know who you've become."

Ishmael smiled.

"I know exactly who I've become," she said. "And now you're going to find out."

8

THE BOAT MOTORED AWAY FROM THE DOCK with Allen at the wheel. Diane sat in the bow and kept one hand on her head to secure her wide-brimmed hat. A shout came from the docks and Diane waved and smiled like she was perched on the lip of a convertible in a parade.

The day was overcast and warm, but Ishmael wore Diane's sunglasses and kept the hood up on one of Allen's sweatshirts. She certainly didn't want anyone to recognize her.

They rode straight out into the Pacific until land was visible, but too distant to be distinct. There were no other boats around. Allen cut the motor, and the boat tossed unevenly in the waves.

"Y'all better hurry this up," Diane said from beneath her hat. "I don't get my sea legs without a heavy dose of Dramamine."

Ishmael stood and walked to the back of the boat. She stripped her clothes and stood naked for a moment on the stern. Allen pretended to be impatient, but Ishmael could feel his eyes on her.

"Here goes," she mumbled to herself and dove in before she had the chance to think.

The water was chilly, but the tingle awakened her. She surfaced, thinking her teeth would be chattering, but instead, she was smiling, glad to be back in the water. She felt freer without a tangled mat of hair weighing her down. The sun broke briefly from the clouds; the warmth of light on her shoulders was like an embrace. She paddled with her arms, dragging her legs behind her.

Allen cranked the motor and idled alongside. She knew he was watching her every move, but she didn't look up. She kept her eyes straight ahead, focused. It was exhilarating to know that in only seconds, two other people would know her secret.

"Ho-ly *shit*, will you look at that?" Diane exclaimed from the boat.

The water was cold, but she felt it now: the wrapping, the stretching in her toes, the bonding of her legs into one. She kicked and felt the force of her fluke behind her. The propulsion. She could hardly imagine the spectacle for the two witnesses gawking over the rail of the boat.

Her body felt so much stronger, so much more competent in this state. She rolled over onto her back and fluttered her tail beside the boat, looking up at Allen and Diane.

Allen beamed back at her, his eyes wide. His face broke into a smile.

"*Unbelievable*," he whispered.

Diane held out her arm to Allen, her eyes fixated on Ishmael. "Pinch me, sugar. Pinch me so I'll wake up."

Allen whistled with amazement. "I certainly had to see it to believe it," he added.

"Doubting Thomas." Diane smacked his arm. "I could've told

you stuff like this was possible. You ever study any quantum mechanics? Sub-atomic particles and what-not? Now *that* is the strange stuff."

Allen was shaky, giddy.

"How? That's—your—it's *incredible*," he said.

"It is," Ishmael responded, looking down at her fluke that had replaced her feet. "I would have to agree that it absolutely is."

Ishmael laughed and then dove beneath the surface and swam straight down. It was remarkable to be able to swim like this. So fast. So strong. She pushed her body deeper until she felt her ears pop, her lungs nearly burst. She looped back toward the surface. The boat above her was just a blurry shadow. She kicked and shot upward toward the sunlight, breaking free of the water at the surface and shooting up into the sky among an explosion of water droplets. She heard Diane shriek with glee, then Ishmael tucked her body in the air and dove back into the water, relishing the silence and the solitude of this new realm that belonged to her.

She swam back to the boat and kicked once with such power that she lifted herself out of the water and perched her body on the edge of the boat. She smiled. There was nothing to say: words were trivial compared to her exhilaration.

Allen gaped at her. "You're—this is—beautiful."

"Note to self," Diane said. "My Harry *has not* been smoking too much of his pipe." She shifted around, looking at Ishmael from all angles. "You really do look pretty darn amazing, darling." She stepped back. "You're glowing. You're in your element." Diane gestured to Ishmael's breasts and whispered, "Are those real? They're so *perky*."

"Ish, I'm—I was a jerk," Allen said. "You were telling the truth. I'm sorry."

"You were. And I was," she said. "But it was an impossible thing to believe. So I forgive you."

"So, wow. Holy shit. What now?" he asked. "Sky's the limit, eh?"

"For starters, I want some more time out here. Would you come back and get me in a few hours?" Ishmael gestured to Diane. "You should take her back to the marina anyway. She's going to get sick out here."

Diane held a handkerchief to her lips, confirming her nausea.

Ishmael wanted some time alone in the water. Time to remember. To ponder. To get clarity. Her mom might be out there. She fell backwards off the boat and splashed back into the water.

When she surfaced, Allen was already yelling. "I can't just leave you out here!"

"Yep. It's official," Diane mumbled. The color had drained from her face. "I feel like a pile of cow dung."

"Go," Ishmael urged. "I'll be fine. You know I will. I've made it this far. I'm practically bulletproof at this point."

"But what if someone sees you?" Allen asked.

"They won't," she said. "I can hold my breath for a pretty long time these days." Her lungs did feel stronger when she was in this form.

"How will I find you?" he asked.

She kicked so that she rose out of the water enough to kiss his cheek.

"You won't have to," she said. "I'll find you."

Falling back with a controlled splash, she tucked and swam away from the boat, farther out to sea. The water rushed beside her as she sped off. Moments later, she heard the start of the motor and then the fading hum of the boat moving in the opposite direction.

9

SHE APPROACHED THE KELP PADDY from underwater and noticed a collection of narrow fish lingering beneath the floating island, flashing their iridescence as they circled under the protective shelter. As she surfaced, gulls were perched atop, resting and preening. It was an oasis of color, rich browns and yellows of the kelp forest combined with the stark alabaster whites of the birds amidst the vast blue.

She lay her head back and floated, catching her breath from the swim and staring at the drifting clouds in the distance. A single gull squawked and flapped its wings; then the flock of gulls lifted off the kelp at once and hovered in the air. She poked her head underwater: the glimmering schools of fish had become skittish as well. As peaceful as she may have felt moments before, she suddenly realized that she was far less acclimated than these creatures.

She dove underwater and swam beneath the kelp bed, peering around. When she surfaced, a few gulls still flapped in the air, but most had landed again. She kicked and rose up enough to tuck her head and dive beneath the surface. This time, she dove straight down, rocketing deeper into the dark water below. Her heart was already pounding. She was getting deeper—deeper than she had ever been. Her lungs were bursting; her eardrums throbbed, but she kept going. She was curious what this new body could accomplish. It felt amazing to push herself like this.

Finally, she turned back. There above her, blocking her path to the surface, was the creature that had scared the gulls off the kelp and had sent the fish scampering. She nearly choked in her body's instinct to gasp.

The ivory belly of a great white shark sliced through the water. A single, simple line for a mouth, hiding rows of jagged teeth. Pointed fins reached out like wings on a fighter jet. The creature was at least three times her size.

Where could she go? What could she do? She would need a breath soon. Hell, she needed a breath now.

She forced her eyes wide. The salinity burned. The shark zigzagged deeper toward her. Its vertical tail pushed side to side like the beat of a metronome, curving its entire massive body to the right, then the left. King of the jungle, lion of the sea. No need to rush.

She couldn't go any deeper; her eardrums would burst. She had to figure a way out of this. Alone. The realization made her head pound. She was seriously out of her league. She hadn't spent her entire life in the ocean like the shark. She was still getting used to this new body.

The shark approached; she thought of all the knives inside that mouth. All the blood that would spill. All the pain. Hopefully it would be over quickly. She hated the thought of struggling, writhing. *Please don't play with your food. Please just eat me and be done with it.* God, she needed to surface. She needed a breath. She was going to explode.

The creature's size increased as it neared.

One bite and there would be nothing left of her. She thought of Allen, searching for her, confused. She hoped he didn't see all the blood. It would be too gruesome.

Desperate for a breath, she couldn't stand it any longer. She swished her fluke hard and pressed toward the sunlight above. The animal darted—faster than she could ever imagine a creature could move. The mouth opened; she saw the rows of triangular teeth out of the corner of her eye—a dark amphitheater of serrated shards. She waited for the bite to pierce her skin, the jaws to crush her.

She heard a shrill chirping. The sound came from nowhere and everywhere. Again, the sound. Distinct. Piercing. The next shrill shriek was followed by a dull thump. And another. Dull thump.

All at once, she was swooped up; she was racing to the surface, then her head broke through the crust like an eggshell cracked and she was in another world, the wind in her face.

She gulped, sucking in her first breath. Her sense of smell restored, the pungent stench of the kelp and bird feathers and fish scales again palpable in her mouth. She looked around. How the—?

She was at the surface. Breathing. Unharmed. Sunlight beat down on her peach-fuzz scalp. Surely the shark would come back for her. She squinted in the brightness and spun in all directions, searching for the trademark fin slicing the water.

She saw something. Near the kelp bed. She wiped her eyes, dove, and swam as fast as she could. Schools of fish parted like draperies in her path. She rose and saw a female hovering in the kelp. She wanted to hug her. She reached out, but the creature jerked away.

"You saved me!" she said, breathless.

The female only stared at her. Her teeth were rugged, the nails on her hands were fiercely long, her hair roughly tangled and ornamented with feathers and shells. She was savage, but not entirely frightening. Surely she had somehow fended off the shark. All the stories Ishmael had ever read about mermaids and all the pictures she had seen in storybooks did this creature no justice. This mermaid in front of her was never going to cover her breasts with starfish or sit on a rock and comb her hair with a shell. This creature was tough. Fierce. The female swam close, right up to Ishmael's face, and reached out as if to grab her hand.

Ishmael instinctively pulled back. She looked at the female curiously.

"What's your name? Can you talk?" she asked. "I'm looking—I'm wondering if you've heard of—my mother."

The female moved her head, but Ishmael wasn't sure whether she was saying no or merely shaking off the question in confusion.

"Anna. Her name is Anna Morgan."

Again, the female moved in and tried to grab Ishmael's arm. Perhaps she wanted to lead her somewhere, but Ishmael wasn't sure she was ready to follow.

Ishmael pulled her hand away. "I want you to say something."

The female clicked back at her. Ishmael tried to watch her face, to read her expressions, to understand.

"I don't—I'm not sure what you're trying to say," Ishmael said.

They hovered in the water, fluttering their tails to keep them upright and stable. The female pointed and Ishmael turned at the female's gesture. All Ishmael could see was the length of the land, expansive behind them.

"What? Land? What are you trying—"

The female struggled out a word. "Ga-aw."

"Gaw?" Ishmael asked. "Gaw? What's gaw?"

The female said the word again, better this time. "Go-ow."

"Go? Go where? Where should I go?"

The female continued to gesture toward land.

"You want me to go? Go back? You want me to go back to land?"

The female only looked at her.

"Go back for what? What am I going back to?"

Still no response. Ishmael sighed.

Go back? To what? A fiancé she's not in love with who thinks she's dead? A slew of paintings that would probably never sell now that she'd screwed her connection with the Santorini Gallery? And Allen? Was he worth going back for?

Wait a second.

Hadn't her dad told her once that she had a grandmother named Maggie who lived on some island. Butter Island? Something like that. In South Carolina.

"Maggie," she said.

The female perked up.

"Maggie?" Ishmael said. "You know something about Maggie?"

The female chirped.

"I'll take that as a 'yes'." Ishmael's brain started to buzz. "*Maggie*," she whispered.

The female watched some birds in the distance. She seemed to be charting where they were diving for fish, planning her next meal.

"That's it? I've got to go to South Carolina? Is that what you're trying to tell me?" She grabbed the female's shoulders. "But I don't have any money. No clothes. No ID. No car. I'm *dead*! I can't go to South Carolina!"

The female jerked and dove, seemingly agitated by Ishmael's sudden excitement. Ishmael let her go, transfixed by this new idea: an idea that might just work. Her grandmother was her mother's mother. Maggie would have some answers.

Ishmael lay on her back and floated, a forearm over her eyes to block the sun. It was amazing how well this new form floated, how buoyant she could be.

How was she going to get to South Carolina? Plane ticket. No. No planes. That would require identification. She wasn't ready to come clean and admit she was alive. That ruled out buses as well. Maybe Allen would drive her. Could she convince him? Of course she could. He was still in love with her.

She heard a noise and shot up. Please, not the shark again. A wave lifted her and she spotted the female in the kelp paddy. The female was picking through the floating field of brown bulbs and leaves, nibbling on whatever was edible. As Ishmael approached, the female held out her hand. Her fingers were thicker than Ishmael's, clawed and weathered liked talons. And yet, there on that feral hand, perched on the pinky finger, was Ishmael's engagement ring.

"That's not a sight you see every day," Ishmael said.

The female took the ring off her finger and shoved it securely into Ishmael's hand.

"Go-w," she said again, her voice untrained like a deaf person. Her mouth stretched out, sort of curved. Was that a smile? And then she went back to picking and eating the critters from the kelp. Ishmael looked down at the ring: a monstrous shimmering diamond set on top of a throne of sapphires. The pale gold band was inlaid with even more sparkling gems.

She secretly hated this ring. Every time she'd been asked to show it to someone, she'd felt ridiculous. She would've preferred a simple band, maybe a custom ring from a local jeweler.

But she could use it . . . *That's it!* This was the money Ishmael needed. Sure, maybe it wasn't the most honest thing to do, but Nicholas thought she was dead. The ring was lost to him. Knowing Nicholas, he'd probably already collected insurance on the thing.

Ishmael looked up to say something to the female—thank her or say goodbye—even if she didn't understand, it was the polite thing to do. But the female was gone, and Ishmael felt a pang.

The sun had dropped lower in the sky. Ishmael turned toward the land and dove. Her body rose and fell as she swam, bouncing rhythmically like a ball across the water, sliding in and out of the waves like a ribbon thread through a swath of silk.

10

SHE SWAM BESIDE THE BOAT and surfaced with a smile. The glistening salt water dripped from her face and made her skin tingle in the afternoon light. She kicked with her tail so that she shot out of the water and perched herself on the edge of the boat.

"Told you I'd find you," she said.

She knew what she looked like to Allen in that moment. With no hair, she was all lips and eyelashes and cheekbones.

"You were driving slow enough," she said. "You were scared you'd run me over, weren't you?"

Allen pulled towels out of a large duffel bag. The playful dimple appeared on his left cheek.

"I wasn't scared," he said. "I was being careful."

She smiled and reached a hand out to touch his arm. "Thanks."

"You're welcome," he said, offering up a towel. "So what do we do now? Dry you off?"

"I guess a towel makes sense, but I'm in no hurry. It's a gorgeous afternoon. Let's take our time. Enjoy it."

He set the towel aside and joined her on the edge of the boat. They sat for a moment, enjoying the setting sun on the water. Ishmael loved the feeling of the salt water air-drying on her skin. She sensed him staring at her and she returned the gaze.

"Ish, you're ripped."

She laughed. "I've been swimming a few laps."

"Can I touch you?" he asked.

Her eyes shot in his direction. Her heart pounded at the thrill of his bluntness, but then she saw his hand reaching out toward what had been her legs.

"My tail? Right. Sure." She lifted her fluke. "Be my guest. Just feels like wet leather to me."

He put his hand on her tail and felt the hide's rubbery wetness.

"Wet leather's a good description," he said. He touched her as if she were a science project. "I hooked up with this chick once from Louisiana who had alligator-skin boots. Felt something like this," he said. "And I touched an eel once when I was spear-fishing. But I guess this seems tougher than an eel's skin." His hand still on her tail, he asked, "What happens to all your organs and stuff?"

"I get the feeling that not much of that has to shift. I mean, the main change happens in my feet and my legs. My lower half gets wrapped up by this extra skin."

She patted the thick skin where her thighs would be.

"I can't help it. I have to ask." He looked at her, still trying to be serious, but a grin was peeking out on his face. "You said you saw a male. So, ah—what's he do about his chorizo con huevos?"

She laughed. "I have no idea." She tilted her head back and watched a flock of birds fly overhead, then turned back to him. "The males I saw in the sea cave didn't have mermen shlongs flopping around. I guess it all just tucks up in there like a whale or something."

"Whoa—does that hurt? Can you feel that?" he asked, pointing to her fluke.

He jerked his hand away and stared in horror as her leathery skin began to transform. The curvature of her individual legs began to appear as the thicker skin dissolved and dripped off her lower half like candle wax. Little fish came to the surface and pecked at the discarded flesh of her tail.

"Is that gross?" she asked, looking at the fish eating her dissolving tail. "Because I'm thinking this could be a major turn off."

"I was just thinking the opposite," he said. "I'm watching a mermaid turn into a naked woman right before my very eyes." He regained composure, pointing to the feeding fish. "Circle of life. At least it's not going to waste."

They watched as the pointed tips of her fluke wilted and the knobs of her ten toes formed as buds on her feet. She held on to the rail of the boat and pried her legs apart. A gooey film pulled between them like a spider web but eventually tore. She wriggled her toes and bent her knees, spinning herself around to drop her feet onto the deck. She stood easily, drying her face with the towel.

"Just like that," he said, aghast at her nonchalance. "What the—you don't have toenails."

"I know. They fell off. But I was never really a pedicure kind of girl anyway. I also don't have any more leg hair. I'm sure you noticed. No more bikini waxes for me," she said with a smile as she started pulling on the clothes that he had brought her. Her teeth were chattering. "See. Here I go. Now I'm starting to get cold. Without my tail, I'm a wimp."

By the way he was looking at her, she was pretty certain he'd already noticed that she was hairless from the waist down.

"So where did it all go?" he asked.

"I don't know. Aquatic animals don't really have hair. It just fell out, I guess. No need for it."

"But you had hair on your head?" he asked. "At least, you did."

"Look, Allen," she said as she pulled his sweatshirt over her head, "I don't have all the answers. This is all new to me too, you know?"

He started fidgeting with the boat's electronics. She knew he would be pacing if they were in a larger space. She could think of numerous times when he had paced around his apartment when their discussions had become too intense for him.

"Did you ever swim with dolphins?" she asked.

"No," he said, barely looking up from the depth finder.

"Me neither," she said.

He waited a second and then threw his hands up. "Yes you have! You just did! You're a mermaid, for chrissakes!"

"Well, sure, yeah, but I'm talking like in Hawaii or Florida or something. Like at a resort." She shrugged. "I thought maybe you had some insight into what they're like. Dolphins. Aquatic mammals." She bit her lip and looked away for a moment, then turned back to him. "I think these mermaid creatures are less human than I would have thought them to be. More animal. More dolphin-like."

"Well, that would make sense. I mean—"

"I saw one," she interrupted.

He froze and looked at her.

"Out there. Today," she said. "A female."

"Did it talk to you? How—what did you say to her?" he asked.

"That's what I'm trying to tell you. She didn't talk. She wasn't really human at all. If she'd talked—I mean, fish don't talk—it would have been strange."

She could see his mind racing.

"*Damn*. Thanks to seasick Diane, I missed out. I can't believe you saw another one," he said. "I want to see *another* one."

"Allen, I think the female was trying to tell me to stay on land. I think that's why they left me on the beach in Baja and didn't keep me in that sea cave."

"How can you possibly know that if she couldn't talk?"

"Well, she did kind of talk. She said 'go.'"

"Go? Go where?"

She looked back at him and swallowed. "Will you help me?"

If there were ever a chance for him to kiss her, this would definitely be the time. She could sense that he felt the connection as well.

"I need answers," she said.

Her eyes were desperate, trusting, pleading. He leaned in closer. She could feel his breath on her own mouth. He nodded, unable to speak. Of course he would help her. He'd do anything for her. She could feel it. The magnetism between them: it was still there. Or was it just the sun setting, the gentle rock of the boat, the salt on her skin? She panicked.

"Take me to South Carolina."

He pulled back. "What?"

"I have a grandmother there. I've never met her. She's my mom's mom. She's got to know something."

She could tell he wasn't ready to let go of the moment quite yet.

"Sure. Of course."

"She lives on some island." She broke away from his attempt at an embrace. "She's my only hope."

He bent his elbows and rubbed the back of his arms.

"Ish, money's a little tight right now—"

A grin broke her face. She lifted her left hand.

"You know that pawn shop off the 5 by the In-N-Out Burger?" she asked.

The diamond on her finger glistened in the fading sunlight.

"Nicholas proposed to you with *that*?" he asked. "That thing's a monster."

His eyes drifted to hers.

"Yeah, I know the one," he said.

She knew he wanted nothing more than to get rid of the ring, take her away with him, and leave Nicholas in the dust.

He smiled back at her. "South Carolina, here we come."

11

"TOOK Y'ALL LONG ENOUGH," Diane yelled once they got close enough to the dock. "What the heck were you two doing out there?"

Allen brought the boat alongside the dock. Despite her tight skirt, Diane took the bowline from Ishmael and bent down to fasten the line to the cleat.

Allen was grinning ear to ear. "What's with the wardrobe change, Johnny Cash? I've never seen you wear that much black."

"I'm not trying to rain on everybody's parade, but I think we better get a move on and figure out some plan of attack here before this little lady becomes a roadside attraction."

"It's cool," Allen said. "We've got a plan."

"Well, the reason I'm wearing this dark attire—that completely washes out my complexion—is because we're supposed to be at a memorial service for the Little Mermaid here in about twenty minutes."

Allen looked down at the board shorts and flip-flops he was wearing.

"It's all good," he said. "We can make that."

"It's in *La Jolla*," Diane said, lifting one eyebrow.

Allen looked at Ishmael.

"La Jolla?" he said, shaking his head. "Here you are, born and raised in Leucadia, and Nicholas holds the memorial service in La Jolla. What's that about?"

Ishmael stepped off the boat. "You know, in another reality, you might have actually liked Nicholas. He's a good guy."

"For starters, I'm not going to that memorial service if it's in La Jolla," Allen said, stepping off the boat. "And secondly, we're headed to the pawn shop."

Allen lifted Ishmael's hand in front of Diane's face.

"Damn-*nation*," Diane said.

Allen dropped Ishmael's hand and checked the lines to secure the boat.

"Pawn shop's a bad idea," Diane said. "You won't get nearly what it's worth. Captain Harry might know some black market guys that—wait, what are you doing that for? Where are we going?"

"We?" Allen asked. "I'm not sure *we* are—"

"South Carolina," Ishmael said.

"Shoot! Why in the heck would we go *there*?"

Allen and Ishmael climbed the metal ramp toward the parking lot. Diane called after them.

"I haven't been back to the South in almost twenty years! And I have no intention of going back to that po-dunk part of the country *now*!"

"Suit yourself," Allen said as he climbed into the truck.

The diesel engine rumbled to a start.

"Well, it sounds like it's just the two of us." Allen said. "You up for this?"

Allen took Ishmael's hand and squeezed it.

"Man, your hands are freezing," he said, rubbing her palm.

Diane rapped on the window. Allen let go of Ishmael's hand.

"I assume this means you're coming with?" he asked.

"*Assume* makes an ass out of you and me," she said. "But I'm sure as hell not driving off by myself to some memorial service for someone I know isn't dead!"

Allen craned his neck out the window and a smile broke his face. "Well, well, well. I see you even packed a bag. How clever of you."

"Listen here, Allen. I realize I'll be taking the backseat on this mission. But y'all are going to need a navigator when you cross over to the other southern coast of the country. So let's play nice. And, yes, I packed a bag. I had a pretty strong suspicion we weren't going to stick around here and let our girl get discovered. I just thought we'd go somewhere fun."

Allen got out of the truck and pulled the seat forward. Diane climbed in, leaving her bag on the ground.

"Oh, don't trouble yourself, Diane. I'll get that for you," Allen said. He carried the suitcase around the back of the truck.

"So, darling, where exactly are we headed?" Diane asked Ishmael as she situated herself in the backseat.

Allen rummaged in the truck-bed camper behind them, organizing.

"Ah, Butter Island, I guess. It's somewhere off the South Carolina coast. I have a grandmother there. My mom's mom."

"Butter Island? What the heck—wait, are you talking about But-*ler* Island?" Diane asked.

"I guess," Ishmael said.

Allen opened the door and climbed into the driver seat.

"Good news," Diane said as soon as he had closed the door. "I've already earned my weight in gold."

Allen looked at her in the rearview mirror.

"Margarine Island—I think that's where you two were headed before I got in the car?" She leaned forward. "Well, now we're heading to a place that actually exists."

Allen looked at Ishmael and then back at Diane in the mirror.

"Butter Island?" he asked. "You know where it is?"

"But-*ler* Island. And yes. Spent three summers in a row there." She crossed her arms and leaned back, knowing she had their attention. Charm bracelets on her arms jingled. "Dated a guy from Butler who worked on a shrimp boat. My parents hated him. Best summers of my life. Forbidden loving is the best loving."

Allen chuckled, sliding the truck into motion. "Wow. And with that, we're off like a prom dress."

"Butler's not exactly a booming metropolis," Diane said. "You know your grandmother's name?"

"Maggie," Ishmael said.

"Then I'm pretty sure we can find her. It's a small world, sugar. Mr. Walt Disney was right."

Allen shifted his eyes to look at Diane in the mirror.

"What's Captain Harry think about you leaving like this?" he asked.

Diane waved Allen off with the flick of her wrist.

"Ah, he don't care. He's headed to Miami first thing tomorrow for some boat show. I was going to fly there next week anyway and meet him. Flights are cheaper out of South Carolina. Plus, he's been saying you needed to get out of town."

"Me? What have I got to do with this?" Allen asked, turning his head to look at her.

Diane pointed to Ishmael with her nail file.

"You've been moping around like a lost puppy since her truck went off the cliff."

Allen accelerated onto the freeway, staring straight into the horizon.

"Diane, how much did you tell Captain Harry?" Ishmael asked. "I mean, you didn't tell him that—"

Diane tucked the nail file in a narrow pocket of her purse. "Why, of course I didn't, sugar," she said, surveying the cover of a glossy magazine she'd pulled out of her purse. When she found a page in the magazine advertising perfume, she opened the scented flap, sniffed it, and then started rubbing the page on her wrists and décolleté.

"Dinner's on me. Should we get sushi for the Little Mermaid or—no, I'm calling in pizza. I'll get double anchovies on half."

Allen turned to Ishmael. "I've got some extra clothes I keep packed away in the camper. If you want, you can change when we stop."

Diane dialed the number to a pizza place. She held the phone to her ear, tilting the receiver away from her mouth.

"Sugar, actually, you need some more—how should I say this—*feminine* looking clothes." She quickly put the phone back to her mouth. "Yes, I'll hold." Covering the mouthpiece with her hand, she whispered, "We'll make sure to find us a shopping mall along the way, honey."

Ishmael looked down at her clothes: a pleated pair of jeans from another decade and a hippie linen shirt that Allen had left in the dryer and shrunk. The sleeves of the shirt barely covered her elbows and, although she had never been much for ironing, she had to admit this shirt was in desperate need of a pressing.

"You look fine, Ish," he said. "Don't listen to her."

Diane pulled a map out of her bag and handed her phone to Ishmael.

"Order whatever you want, darling. I'm paying. I just hate being on hold."

Ishmael took the phone, and the whine of the hold music drifted into her ear.

"Just don't give them your name," Allen said to Ishmael. "Give them mine or Diane's."

"Good thinking. Name like yours doesn't exactly blend in," Diane said, looking at the map. "There's nothing I like about Texas. So let's take the 8 out east and move up north through Phoenix to pick up the 17 north, Then make our way to the 40 and head east. Where are we stopping tonight anyway?" Diane flipped the map over. "Albuquerque. Amarillo. Memphis. Birmingham. I-26. Once we get to Charleston, I can surely pick my way to the Butler Island Bridge."

"You always carry a map of the US in your purse?" Allen asked.

"Oh, you wouldn't believe the preparedness of this little Girl Scout," Diane said. "You never know when adventure's going to call."

The man came back on the other end of the line; Ishmael began to order.

"I told you she'd want anchovies," Diane said. "Didn't I say that?"

Ishmael hung up, passing the phone back to Diane.

"Look, Diane, once we pawn this ring, we're not exactly going to be on the sly anymore," Allen said. "I'm going to make a few phone calls when we stop. A guy I used to be in business with, his cousin works at the pawnshop. I'm sure he'll take the ring no questions asked, but—"

"So we're moving into sneak mode," Diane said with a wink. "Gotcha."

Diane put a stick of gum in her mouth. Ishmael watched her out of the corner of her eye as Diane folded the stick perfectly on her tongue. Just like a commercial.

"I'm going to rest up for a bit. Whoo-wee. All this coming back from the dead and mermaid excitement's got this little lady plum pooped."

"You're putting gum in your mouth right before you fall asleep?" Allen asked.

"Damn, Allen, you sound like a granny! Does he talk to you like this, Ishmael?"

All the time when we were dating, Ishmael thought.

Diane started fluffing a sweatshirt of Allen's she'd found in the back; she pressed it against the window and leaned on it.

"Don't you worry your handsome little head," she said, as she adjusted her seat belt and closed her eyes. "Listen to whatever music you want. I can sleep through a hurricane. Anywhere and through anything, that's what my Harry always says."

Stars had just begun to appear, white glimmers scattered across the purple-grey sky. The truck bumped along in silence as Diane dozed off. Suddenly, Allen reached across and took Ishmael's hand, kissing the inside of her wrist. She jerked her hand away.

"What?" Allen whispered. "I was holding your hand less than twenty minutes ago."

"I was cold."

"Well, that kiss you gave me on the boat wasn't cold."

"What? The peck on the cheek?"

Ishmael saw Diane slitting her eyes so that she could catch a visual of the scene.

"Don't worry. I'm still asleep. Not listening," Diane said.

"That's what it was to you?" Allen asked. "A peck?"

Allen looked hard at Ishmael and then turned his eyes back to the road.

"Allen, I said yes when another man asked me to marry him. Clearly I'm not in love with *you* anymore."

Diane gasped.

"*Sorry*," Diane said when they both glanced back at her. "This is better than my soaps."

"Clearly," Allen said. He shifted and looked over at Ishmael. "Clearly, since you popped by my apartment with no clothes on this morning. Clearly, since we're off to the pawnshop to pawn your engagement ring."

Ishmael took a deep breath.

"Allen, I appreciate this," she said. "I appreciate you. You were the only one I could trust not to ship me off to a psychiatric ward or Sea World. No one else would have done this for me. Let's just—let's not do this tonight. Let's not get in a fight."

"I think you should get your own room when we stop at the hotel tonight."

Ishmael shot a look at him, amused. A broad smile swept across her face.

"You actually thought we were going to sleep together tonight?" She stared at him even harder. "Seriously?"

Allen didn't answer. Eyes on the road.

Ishmael shook her head and huffed out an incredulous laugh.

"Did it ever cross your mind that I might have come to you because at one point in time you were my dad's best friend? We're like family, Allen. We should never have crossed that line."

"*We* crossed a line? I think it's you. You've gotten in over your head."

"Well, then, it's a good thing I'm a mermaid," she said.

Allen pulled into the pizza place, slammed into park, and loudly shut the door. The inside of the truck fell to silence.

Ishmael was fuming: she wasn't sure whether she wanted to kiss Allen or slap him. She rubbed a hand across her buzzed scalp.

"I know you're awake, Diane," Ishmael said after a moment in the quiet.

"You're doing the right thing, sugar."

"I know I am," Ishmael said. "Doesn't make it easy though."

"He's heartbroken," Diane said, sitting up. "You know that, right?"

"Yeah, well, I care about him." Ishmael looked off for a moment, but then brought her attention back into the truck. "And we all know after what I've been through; I could stand to get laid." She took a deep breath. "But I've got to keep a clear head. Not get side-tracked."

"That-a girl."

"Whatever lies ahead is all mine to deal with. I don't need anyone holding my hand through all this."

Ishmael glanced out the window.

"Here he comes," Ishmael said, cracking open the door. "I'm going to ride in the back."

"I'll pass a slice or two back to you," Diane said, reading Ishmael's mind.

Ishmael climbed into the camper, which was a sea of blankets. Allen had laid out two sleeping bags and tossed a few pillows back there as well. She needed to get some rest. Even from the back, as soon as Allen opened the door, she caught a whiff of cheese melting on warm dough. She distinctly smelled the anchovies, suddenly aware of her hunger.

"Where'd she go?" she heard Allen ask.

"She's riding in the camper, darling," Diane answered. "We figured that was the safest place for her. You know, in case we get pulled over or anything. Don't want anyone recognizing the dead girl we've got riding around with us."

Ishmael was suddenly grateful Diane was along for the journey.

A sound of shuffling pizza boxes, and Diane tapped on the sliding window between the truck and the camper, passing back an entire pizza box with napkins on top. Diane winked at Ishmael, then slid the window shut.

Ishmael heard Diane moving into the front seat, seatbelts buckling.

"What do you say to rushing this special delivery?" Diane asked.

Ishmael peeked through the curtain between the camper and the cab of the truck.

"Drive straight on through. Cross country like Kerouac. I'll grab us some energy drinks at the next gas station."

"Yeah. Sure," he said.

"Allen, beneath all that confidence, you know she's afraid." Diane lowered her voice to a whisper. "Her life's been turned upside down."

Allen cranked the car and then pressed the gas pedal, revving the engine.

"And you don't think mine has?" he asked.

"You're being selfish."

Allen struck the steering wheel with the palm of his hand and then looked over at Diane.

"Am I?"

Ishmael admired his tousled hair through the slit in the curtain. She had to admit, he looked handsomely tortured in the moment.

"Sugar, I can think of far worse things," Diane said. She put a hand on his shoulder. "Now let's get this mermaid to the Atlantic before she dries out."

PART TWO

East Coast

12

Slowly rounding the last turn, the truck navigated the dirt road toward number 38 White House Road, an address obviously stemming from the fact that it was the only house at the end of the road—and it was white. Thirty-eight ancient oak trees lined the road, nineteen on each side, left over from pre-Civil War days when the property had been a magnificent plantation with rice fields and slave quarters.

The house, built before hurricane building codes, was two storied but sat low to the ground, vulnerable to floodwater, and was topped with a gabled roof that was known to act like a sail in the high winds of a seasonal gale. The roof miraculously hadn't been ripped off, and number 38 stood sturdy and unscathed.

The truck pulled to a stop in a cloud of dust, and Ishmael rose from her cocoon in the camper to peer out the window. Overflowing potted plants were scattered all over the property, growing vibrant and untrimmed. A garden was off to one side in the only spot of the dirt yard not shaded by the sweeping oak trees. A tall woman with deep walnut skin swept the back steps in the shadow of these trees: there was something arresting about the way she moved in the dappled light, her apron strings swaying with her movements. Ishmael grabbed the art supplies Allen had bought for her in Albuquerque and turned to a fresh page in her sketchbook.

Diane got out of the truck, adjusting her shirt, and immediately started to apply lipstick in the side mirror. She and Allen obviously hadn't noticed the woman.

Ishmael peeked out the window, blowing on the page to get rid of the charcoal residue. Her hand slid across the paper, a character coming to life with swift, dark lines. The woman was hefty, sturdy like a tugboat. Her hair was short, wiry, and winter white—a dust of snow cresting on a mountain of a woman. Ishmael admired her quick rendition and set the sketchbook aside just as the woman on the steps rested her broom against the banister.

"I feel so rude," Diane said. She fixed her hair in the mirror and then tossed the lipstick in her purse and shut the door. "Not calling ahead. How do people not have a phone these days?"

Ishmael climbed out of the camper, squinting in the white afternoon light.

The woman on the steps crossed her arms over her large breasts. It was apparent she wasn't expecting any visitors.

"Thank y'all kindly for stopping by, but this here ain't no motel."

The woman's voice was strong. The words came out thick, like blackstrap molasses—bitter but good for you.

"Oh my! How do you do?" Diane fluttered right in with all her Southern charm once she saw the woman. "Name's Diane Dunaway. And this here is Allen Wilson."

The woman on the steps didn't move or speak.

Diane giggled nervously, "Our apologies for showing up

unannounced. We're looking for the grandmother of our friend here. Any chance you're hiding a long-lost grandmother in that lovely house of yours?"

Diane pushed Ishmael closer to the woman on the steps.

"Lord, have mercy," the woman whispered, staring at Ishmael. "Good-*ness* be."

The woman came down the steps. She got right in Ishmael's face, studying it. She was taller than Ishmael and much heavier, with muscle and thick skin. An intimidating presence.

"You're Anna and Richard's girl," the woman said. "I see it in those eyes. No hair on that head of yours, but I figure it'd be like your momma's if there was. Color of a yellow raspberry."

"You knew my mother?" Ishmael asked. She was ecstatic, hope rising in her chest.

"Why sure, child. I knew your momma and daddy when you were just an angel up in heaven waiting to come on through. I've been with Maggie a *long* time."

The woman stepped back and grinned wide. Her tone changed completely as she spoke again—she nearly giggled.

"Leon—he sent word by some boy pedaling a bicycle like he was on fire. Boy tell me we got us a package coming." Her deep laugh seemed to shake the air around her. "I couldn't for the *life* of me figure out what could be so important that Leon would send a boy on a bike pedaling that cut-through in the woods."

Ishmael relaxed at the change in the woman's tone.

"Name's Lena," she said. "Y'all come on in and I'll get you something to drink." She turned her bulky frame and marched up the steps, talking over her shoulder. "Lord Almighty, this is a big day. A big day, indeed."

She held the screen door open, smiling at them as they entered.

"It hot like the devil himself outside. But that breeze'll pick up. Later in the day it'll come on through and cool us right off."

She offered them a seat at the kitchen table, her deep and reverent humming filling the room while she retrieved a glass pitcher from the fridge. Round yellow lemon slices floated in the dark liquid. The kitchen smelled candied and succulent, like an orchard basking in the sun.

Allen took a seat at the table, glassy-eyed after the traveling. Diane seemed to be in her element, complimenting Lena on the house and offering to help in any way she could. Ishmael surveyed the room, trying to fit herself into this house that was somehow a piece of her history.

"Maggie's on a walk," Lena said, filling three glasses she'd put on the table. "We've got us a few hive boxes under them pecan trees, so we check on them time-to-time. That's our own honey I use to sweeten that tea y'all are sipping. Good, ain't it? Y'all staying for supper? Making fried okra, and I got us a pecan pie in the oven." She pronounced pecan as *pee-can*.

"Why, that would be lovely, Lena! Thank you," Diane answered for the group as she sat down at the table. "I was wondering what smelled so good in this kitchen. And this tea is just de*lish*ous."

Ishmael wanted to laugh at Diane's syrupy politeness, but she was grateful someone was taking the reins. She was in no mood for chit-chat now that she'd crossed the country and was sitting in her grandmother's house.

"Tell us, Lena," Diane said, "where should we get a hotel room around these parts?"

"Ho-*tel*? No, Diane. Y'all stay here tonight. We've got plenty of room."

"Well that will be lovely. Won't that be lovely, y'all?"

Diane walked across the room and winked at Ishmael as she yanked a tissue from a box on the counter and wiped the sweat from her upper lip and brow. Lena had her back turned toward the sink but seemed to sense exactly what the tissue was being used for.

"Flip that switch over there—in the corner there," she said. "I'm used to the heat by now so I always forget to turn that on."

Allen flipped the switch, and the overhead fan spun to life. Ishmael immediately felt the relief of the breeze cooling the sweat on her skin.

"I don't know how you do it, Lena," Allen said, pulling his shirt in and out to fan his chest. "I've never felt heat like this in my life."

"Oh, you get used to it. Got no need to have that fake air-conditioning sealing us up in this house. This is just a still time a day. Like I said. Tide changes and the breeze'll come on through."

Lena went back to humming as she moved her cumbersome frame about the kitchen. She was completely relaxed, even with these last-minute visitors suddenly in her kitchen.

"Y'all are so tucked away," Diane said. "It's so nice and peaceful."

"And private! No phone, no TV, no radio, and no paper! The mailman don't even come down this road! Maggie likes quiet, and she figure if anything important is going on, Leon'll tell us."

"And Leon hasn't said anything lately about Ishmael?" Diane asked.

Lena's back was turned; she looked out the window over the sink as she snapped the tops off beans and divided her work into different bowls.

"None I heard, Diane. Been slow round here lately. August is so hot we don't get nothing done." She turned around, smiling. "Why? We got us a wedding or something?" She turned back to the window. "Everybody like a wedding. But around here at this time, with it being so hot, we don't get—"

Diane choked on her tea. "Can I trouble you, Lena, for a restroom?"

"Right down the hall thataways," Lena motioned with a handful of beans. "Second door on the right."

Diane left the room and Lena went back to chatting.

"Y'all ladies gonna have to both sleep in that bedroom with the ceiling fan or else one of you'll have to sweat it out in that small room. Somebody might as well sleep on the porch. We got a cot. That bed is mighty nice and cool if you don't mind the bugs tap-tapping on them screens all night."

"The guest room sounds perfect," Ishmael said, feeling like she had to say something. "We're glad to share a room. Thank you."

She got up and walked over to the window. Allen joined her, sipping his tea and looking out at the dock and the creek.

"Gorgeous piece of property you've got here," he said.

"We think so," Lena said, looking at the same view out the other window over the sink. "Glad y'all here to share it."

A modern dock house cantilevered out over the water, poised over the marsh grass on its wooden stilts like a great blue heron. The grass gently swayed at the slightest breeze, and the majestic old oaks swept out over the creek, casting elegant shadows on the water.

Something caught Lena's eye out the window and she craned her thick neck to get a better look through the slit in the curtain. She turned to Allen. "You're gonna have to excuse me—I'm getting tripped up on that name of yours. Keep wanting to call you *Woodrow* for some reason."

"Allen. No worries. Last name is Wilson."

"Woodrow Wilson! Thought I was about going crazy. Knew there was something in there with a 'W!'" Lena laughed and her eyes softened to slits as her cheeks rose with a wide smile. "Woowhee. You see that boat coming up the creek yonder?"

Allen nodded.

"That'd be Hector. He lives in the dock house and he must be having some engine troubles because he's out there paddling those oars like a fool. Take him some beers, if you will. You two can have some man-time and discuss fixing that crazy good-for-nothing boat of his."

"Sure—sure—of course," Allen said, springing to action.

Lena laughed at his hastiness. "Lord, you must be happy to get some male company after being cooped up in that truck with them hens for so long."

Lena opened the fridge and retrieved the beers. Moments later, the screen door slammed and Ishmael watched Allen walk across the yard toward the dock, waving at the man in the boat. She could almost hear their muffled voices and the crack of the beer cans. She felt a twinge of jealousy. Men had it so easy. A female chance encounter like that would have involved far more time before it became that relaxed.

"Lena, you sure there's nothing we can do to help you with supper?" Diane asked, reentering the room.

"I'm fine. Y'all go on and get cleaned up. Make yourself right at home. The guest bedroom with the ceiling fan is down the hall past the bathroom. We keep those two twin beds in there made up with clean linens. Towels are in there by the commode."

Lena picked up a knife and started peeling a tomato. Her fingers were thick, but she wielded the knife with ease. The bright red rind fell like confetti in the porcelain sink.

"Let's get a move on, sugar," Diane said to Ishmael. "You should get cleaned up before you meet your grandmother."

Ishmael stood her ground. She wasn't about to leave the kitchen until her grandmother returned.

Lena shifted bowls around, her hands keeping busy in the sink. "I know it's hard, child," Lena said. "To lose your momma so young and have your daddy just drive off like he did. And now you're about to meet your grandmamma. That's enough to make the heart pound something crazy."

Lena looked out the window and took a deep breath.

"But Maggie—she's got answers for you. You got family now, child. Don't you worry. You got family now."

Lena went back to humming. A voice called from the back porch.

"Lena! You won't believe what I found!"

The back screen door slammed, and a woman rounded the corner in a wide-brimmed sun hat, her hair swaying behind her in a long white braid. The woman pulled the hat off her head and set it on the table, turning slightly. Just enough. Ishmael caught a glimpse of her profile—the eyes, the slight smile, the chin—and she knew exactly who it was.

13

THE MOMENT CHANGED ISHMAEL. Her heart thundered in her chest. She was in the room with her own blood. She instantly felt the connection.

Maggie, breathless with her news, didn't seem to notice the guests in the room.

"A whole *field* of zinnias are still blooming on the back lot! I'd forgotten we'd planted all those seeds in the spring. Our bees were *all* over them!"

"Well, that sure is some good news, Maggie. But we got some company," Lena said.

With a colorful bouquet of flowers in one hand, Maggie was on tiptoe trying to retrieve a vase from a high shelf.

"I saw the truck. Friend of Hector's?" Her voice was strained. She couldn't reach the vase and gave up.

"No, Maggie." Lena nodded in Ishmael's direction. "Good friend of *yours*."

Ishmael's pulse quickened as her grandmother turned and gazed at her, holding the flowers in one hand, covering her mouth with the other.

"My *word*," Maggie said, softly, as if not to disrupt the perfection of the moment. "Ishmael?"

Ishmael stood still. All eyes turned to her. Her heart pounded in her ears.

Maggie crossed the room slowly, as if in a trance. As she walked past Lena, Lena took the flowers from her hand, and snatched the vase off the high shelf, filling it with water.

"You look *just* like her," Maggie said. "Just like my Anna."

Ishmael was suddenly swept up in her grandmother's arms, her own arms pinned at her sides. Maggie kept the embrace short—nothing too intense, as if she didn't want to overdo it—then stepped back and patted Ishmael's upper arms. Ishmael's heart sank as her grandmother's soft hands slipped off her skin.

"I've waited a long time for this moment," Maggie said. "We have a lot of catching up to do." She looked back at Lena, who nodded. "Lena and I would love for you all to stick around for as long as you like."

"I'd . . . sure," Ishmael said. She felt ready to explode with questions but didn't think she'd make much sense right now. "I do have a lot to, ah—to talk to you about."

Maggie smiled, a slight tilt to her head.

"I'm sure you do. And we'll get around to all that—but you do look just like your mother. You're as lovely as she was. I miss her terribly."

Ish saw genuine longing on Maggie's face. She *had* to ask.

"So—where are . . . the photos of her?"

Shoot. Did that sound rude?

"I mean, I didn't see . . . "

Diane stepped up to them. "Maggie, it's so nice to meet you. Name's Diane Dunaway and the pleasure is all mine. We've come a long way. I'm sure Ishmael's just tuckered out."

"No, no. It's okay." Maggie shook Diane's hand. "She's right. It's just . . . pictures make me sadder than anything else. And I don't want to be sad. So I took them all down. Does that make any sense?"

Everyone waited for Ishmael to speak.

"I guess. Yeah, it does," Ishmael said. She thought of the empty walls of the trailer when she was growing up. "Dad and I took all the pictures of her down when she was gone too. I always thought we'd put them back up one day. We, ah—we never did."

"Your mother was a remarkable woman. It was a shame she had to leave this place at such a young age." Maggie looked into Ishmael's eyes. "This is just such a nice surprise. Such a marvelous surprise."

The screen door slammed, and seconds later Allen walked into the room with wet hair, obviously having gone for a swim in the creek.

"Smells even better in this house than I remembered!" he said, joining everyone in the kitchen. "And did I hear someone talking about sticking around for a bit? I'm all in. This place is incredible."

Allen looked over and noticed the silver-haired woman for the first time. Ishmael could see the recognition developing in his expression.

"Wow," he said. "You're Maggie, aren't you?"

"I am," she said with a smile, reaching out a hand.

Allen crossed the room and shook Maggie's hand.

"Well, you're a lovely treasure to find at the end of our hunt," he said. "Not to be rude, but I'm seriously not going anywhere until someone forces me back down that dirt road. You've got an amazing place here. Warm water, the marsh, the dock, the trees. I'm in heaven."

These were the moments when Ishmael admired Allen: he was already as relaxed around Maggie as if she were his own grand-mother. His presence was comforting.

"You three are welcome to stay for as long as you like. Unless—are there more of you? We might not have enough beds!"

"Just the three, Maggie. We're fine. Ain't this a glorious day…" Lena said.

Maggie beamed over at her granddaughter. Ishmael smiled back weakly, overwhelmed.

Another man came in the room. Ishmael hadn't even heard the door slam this time. Hector was younger than he'd looked from afar. He seemed about Ishmael's age. Broad, bare chest, only a towel around his waist, fresh from a swim in the creek. His sable black hair hung down below his shoulders and was tied back in a loose ponytail. His skin was the rich color of caramel. He snatched a slice of tomato from the plate Lena was arranging. Lena playfully smacked Hector's hand.

"Well, well, well . . ." Diane sang, eyeing Hector. "Who is *this*?"

"With no shirt on! In my kitchen!" Lena bellowed. "Boy, you better put some clothes on!"

"I'd say he looks fine just the way he is," Diane said.

Hector beamed back at Diane with a charming grin.

"Diane. Ishmael. This is Hector," Maggie said. "He's our resident male. He lives in the dock house, but you wouldn't know it for all the meals he shares with us up here in the big house."

Hector nodded. "Nice to see y'all." He gestured to the newly filled vase on the windowsill. "Like the zinnias, Maggie. I see you discovered the back field."

"You knew about that field?" Maggie thrust her hands onto her hips. "Hector, you've got to remind us old ladies when we forget where we planted our seeds!"

"I knew you'd find them," he said, reaching over to dip his finger in whatever it was Lena was stirring in a bowl.

"Git!" Lena spun so the bowl was out of reach. "Alright, Maggie, it's time to clear out my kitchen! I've got work to do. And take this fool in the towel with you."

Lena cut her eyes at Hector, but he simply put a hand on her shoulder and kissed her cheek. He went to the fridge and retrieved two cold beers, offering one to Ishmael.

"No. Ah—thanks. I'm good," Ishmael said.

Hector gestured the second beer toward Allen and then tossed the can across the room.

"Well, I'm sure everyone's hungry, and I know Lena has quite a spread for us," Maggie said. "I'll open some champagne and we can celebrate on the front porch. I'm sure I have a bottle hiding around here somewhere."

"I got it all under control. Y'all just give me my space," Lena said.

"Hector, you better go put on some clothes before Lena has a fit," Maggie said, searching through a cabinet. She looked up for a moment toward Allen. "Shower's right down the hall. Help yourself, if you want." She paused and turned around, touching Ishmael's arm. "I'd be honored if my granddaughter would join me on the porch for a celebration toast." She turned back to her search and talked over her shoulder. "Oh, here I am being all forward . . . Do you even drink champagne, Ishmael? There's so much I don't know about you."

"I, ah, I love champagne."

"Good. Me too." Maggie winked. "Do you still swim, dear?"

Yeah, I swim. Ishmael's heart pounded at the question.

Maggie spun around with champagne glasses in her hand.

"I was only asking because your mother was such an avid swimmer. And I knew you won a few trophies back in middle school before you quit the team. Your father sent me a newspaper clipping about that."

"Oh, you mean competitively?" Ishmael asked, playing off her delayed response. "Not anymore." She turned the tea glass she still held in her hand. "My father wrote you letters?"

Maggie struggled with the cork in the bottle, and Lena came over to help her.

"How we thinking we should set the table, Maggie? Y'all want to eat out on the porch?" Lena asked. "Should be a mighty fine night."

The conversations all around Ishmael trailed off into background noise. Ishmael suddenly felt as if she were watching the scene from afar. It felt surreal to be here, standing in her grandmother's kitchen, in South Carolina.

"Hang in there, champ. I know it's overwhelming, but I've got your back."

It was Hector. He'd snuck up behind her, whispered in her ear. He moved away and grabbed the dishtowel from Lena's shoulder, snapping the cloth playfully near Lena's arm. Lena spun around, pointing her finger at him, a smile barely concealed on her face.

"Get on outta here! And put some clothes on!" Lena shouted.

"As you wish," Hector said, throwing the towel back onto Lena's shoulder just before he left the room.

Ishmael moved closer to the window. She watched Hector glide across the lawn, his skin glistening in the sunlight.

Diane took hold of Ishmael's arm and squeezed it lightly. "You seem a little flushed there, darling."

"It's just hot in here," Ishmael said, yanking her arm away

and fanning her face with her hand.

"That's why I'm putting you on ice duty. Cool you down."

Diane shoved a bucket into Ishmael's hands. She turned to the window and the two women watched as Hector navigated his way down the dock.

"And I can see why you're all hot and bothered," Diane added. "But you better look out. Because a man like *that*—who's single— has got to have some sort of baggage."

14

ISHMAEL FOLLOWED DIANE ONTO THE PORCH with the ice bucket. The space was expansive, with a hammock at one end and a long table with benches on either side. Candles were scattered about in hurricane lanterns, their wicks safely sheltered from the evening breezes. At the other end of the porch, an arrangement of wicker furniture with cozy cushions and plush pillows beckoned.

Lena was right. The breeze had picked up. The porch felt amazing.

"Well, this is just delightful!" Diane said.

Maggie started pouring champagne into a glass.

"Goodness!" Diane exclaimed. "Not like me to pass on champagne, but there's a hot shower with my name on it."

"Help yourself," Maggie said. "I'd be delighted to have Ishmael all to myself."

Diane disappeared back into the house, and Ishmael nestled into a chair, preparing all the questions she had in her head. This was the moment she'd been waiting for: she wanted to make sure she used her time wisely. She realized she was still holding the ice bucket and leaned forward to set it next to a stack of books on the coffee table. The top title caught her eye.

"*Finding Your Inner Fish*," she read aloud.

"Fabulous title, isn't it?" Maggie said as she filled a second glass. "An old friend gave me that book. I thought it would be about how we're all fish at heart. But it's more paleontology. Fossils and comparative anatomy and what-not." She held the green bottle daintily at the top of the skinny neck and dropped it in the ice bucket. Passing a glass to Ishmael, she added, "Which is fascinating in its own right, but not exactly what I'd hoped for. Certainly more Hector's cup of tea than mine."

Maggie smiled at Ishmael. She held up her glass. "To Ishmael. My only granddaughter. For making the long trek to come see her old grandmother."

Ishmael felt strange, toasting herself, especially since her grandmother was standing and she was seated.

Maggie reached down to clink her glass and then settled into a chair across from Ishmael with a light sigh. Her long braid lazily draped down the armrest like a silver serpent at ease with its mistress. Maggie sipped her champagne and looked out beyond the porch.

Ishmael followed her gaze. Even though the breeze had picked up a bit, the creek was as still as a sleeping dog. Only if she paid close attention could she see the slightest shifting as it breathed with the current. The oak trees swept their moss-covered branches out over the marsh, gracefully poised as if they were presenting the creek to onlookers.

"Gorgeous, isn't it? The lacy bit hanging from the branches is called Spanish moss." Maggie said. "They're all dancers to me, those oak trees. Flamenco. Frozen mid-dance. I see the moss as those wonderful fringed shawls they wear."

"Is that why it's called Spanish moss?" Ishmael asked.

"No," Maggie said, maintaining her reverie. "But it should be." She gestured to a certain tree with her glass. "That one. See how she just finished. She's in a deep bow. A curtsy to the creek." She took a sip and then turned back to Ishmael.

"I always hoped you'd make the trip to come see me. I've dreamed of this moment many times. I wanted to meet you in the flesh. Pictures were never enough."

"So why didn't you come to see me?" Ishmael felt the twinge of anger in her voice. She blurted out the question without thinking. She regretted her tone, but not the question.

"I can see you're just like your mother—very direct. I'm glad."

"I want to know everything you can tell me about my mother."

"Well, then. I won't bore either of us a moment longer with small talk."

Maggie shifted straighter in her chair and set her glass down.

"For starters, I know what happened to you in Baja," Maggie said.

Ishmael was speechless, flustered.

"I know you had a tail instead of legs that night," Maggie continued, "and I know you escaped those fishermen and swam home in your aquatic form."

Maggie sat back in her chair.

Ishmael knocked over her champagne; the glass caught an edge and shattered. Ishmael moved instinctively to clean it up, but then paused mid-reach and looked up, hypnotized by her grandmother's words. Maggie remained statuesque in the chair, not bothered at all by the mess.

"How could you possibly—?" Ishmael asked.

"Our kind stays connected. News gets passed along."

Lena appeared in the doorway, wiping her hands with a towel. "You two doing alright out here?" She looked down at the puddle. "Don't you go cutting yourself on glass now, Ishmael."

Lena yelled into the house, "Hector, can you bring us a broom?"

Hector appeared from inside the house with a broom and dustpan. He must have slid in the back door. He seemed to just keep appearing out of nowhere and everywhere. As he cleaned the floor, he grinned at her.

"Maggie making you nervous?" he asked.

Diane was right. *Damn.* There was certainly something arresting about him. He reminded her of someone, some famous actor or something.

"You want another glass, Ishmael?" Lena asked, returning to the porch with paper towels and a spray bottle. She handed the cleaning supplies to Hector and started sweeping.

"No. I'm fine. Sorry to make such a mess."

"Oh, please. Not to worry. Let's get you another glass," Maggie said, rising from her chair. "I'm not going to celebrate alone."

Hector finished cleaning while Maggie retrieved the champagne glass that had been meant for Diane. Hector directed one more smile in Ishmael's direction before following Lena through the doorway. After passing the refilled fresh glass to Ishmael, Maggie returned leisurely to her wicker throne. Ishmael sat back and rubbed the fuzz of hair on her scalp, her mind spinning.

Maggie sat still and waited calmly, giving Ishmael the space to speak. The afternoon light streaming through the screens gave her an ethereal glow. Ishmael looked to her grandmother, not sure what to ask first.

"Listen, if you know about what happened—like, *seriously*, you know about Baja—then by all means, fill me in. Because I'm at a loss for an explanation."

"Ishmael, let's just get this out in the open before we're interrupted again." Maggie sat even straighter in her chair. "You're what you might call a *mermaid*." She said the last word with reluctance. "I think that term is foolish. I only use it to get the point across. Basically, you were born of aquatic parents and—"

"Hold up—*what*? Both my parents were mermaids?"

"Well, clearly Richard wasn't a mer-*maid*," Maggie said. "They came to shore to birth you when your mother was nineteen. She returned to the ocean when you were six because—well—she missed the water. She needed it."

Maggie relaxed as if she was relieved at the revelation.

"She returned to the ocean?" Ishmael asked.

"Precisely."

Just like that, confirmed. Ishmael stared blankly at her grandmother for a moment.

"Because she *missed* the water?" Ishmael finally asked.

Maggie nodded.

Ishmael forced a loud exhale. *But she didn't miss her only child?*

"So my mom didn't drown," Ishmael said, watching her grandmother closely to observe every facial cue.

"Oh, you never really believed that, did you?" Maggie asked. "Richard told you the truth. It was a stretch, sure. A big stretch, in fact, for you to hear the truth at such a young age, but he gave you the truth regardless. That way it was always there for you to believe or not." Maggie leaned forward. "Ishmael, your mother is very much alive."

Ishmael felt the tears forming in her eyes, but with the warming of her heart came the swirl of skepticism. She sat forward and looked straight at Maggie.

"*Alive*? Are you sure? *My mom*?"

"Yes. My daughter."

In that moment, relief and love overcame any anger or doubt Ishmael had been holding onto. She sat back. She trusted her grandmother's tone; she felt the words to be truth. And she realized she'd always felt the truth deep inside.

"I mean, I had a feeling, but I wasn't sure." Ishmael took a deep breath. "I certainly didn't really think—I don't know. Wow. Where is she? Can I see her?"

"I'd hoped you would be excited," Maggie said.

"I'm not sure excitement's the right—yeah, I guess I'm excited. But also confused. My whole life so far has been based on lies."

Maggie sipped her champagne. "Richard told you the truth. That should be good news."

Ishmael stood. "I think I have to decide for myself whether this is good news or not. I mean, I was *six* when my dad told me about my mom. And he certainly never brought it up again or gave me any more concrete details."

"Please, sit down," Maggie insisted. "*Relax*. Drink your champagne. And—don't take my bluntness as a lack of compassion."

Ishmael remained standing. "Oh, you're compassionate all right. My mother must have gotten that from you." She stopped and sucked in a long breath. "Look—I'm sorry, Maggie. It's just, all the years of not knowing . . ."

"Anna left you with your father. You were safe and secure. You lived a very nice life, far better than a lot of children get."

Ishmael wasn't sure she liked her grandmother's tone. She paced for a few moments and then finally sat back down.

"Why didn't she ever contact me?" Ishmael questioned.

"The ocean doesn't exactly have phone lines or a postal service. She'd chosen the water over the land—"

"Over her daughter, you mean."

"As I mentioned earlier in the kitchen, your mother's an extraordinary swimmer. And a remarkable diver, I might add. She's much more useful in the water."

"So that's it? She chose the ocean over her *family*?" Ishmael asked.

"Oh, Ishmael—it's much more complicated than you can imagine." Maggie sighed. "Frankly, I was expecting you to be a basket case when you first arrived. And now, I see that you are."

Ishmael scowled and turned away, the adoration she had felt for her grandmother earlier that afternoon dissolving.

"Leaving was a strong, natural instinct for your mother," Maggie said.

"Where is she?" Ishmael asked curtly.

"I don't know."

"*You don't know?*" Ishmael gaped at Maggie. "You're telling me my mother's alive, but you don't know where she is?"

"That's a big ocean out there," Maggie said, gesturing toward the water beyond the porch. "Your mother likes to roam. She's— migratory is probably the wrong word. Let's say she's *nomadic*."

"So even if she is alive, it doesn't matter," Ishmael said. "Because there's no way I can possibly find her."

"There are those who know her whereabouts—I'm just not one of them. She and I don't have any sort of close relationship like you would imagine. I didn't raise her."

"Great. So we have a tradition in our family of mothers deserting their daughters."

Maggie leaned forward. "I came to land pregnant with your mother *fifty years ago* and took her back to the water once she was born. I never deserted your mother—I simply wanted her raised in the water. Where I thought she belonged."

"So you gave her away and never saw her again?"

"I thought I would visit her more often." Maggie looked away. "But it wasn't possible."

Lena arrived in the doorway.

"We're done in the kitchen and I'm heading up to read my book. I made up the cot for Allen. He keeps saying he needs some kind of power nap—whatever that is. I asked him, 'Why you wanna power your way through a nap?'" Lena paused for a moment. "I think he got what I was saying. He's snoring like a bear in winter. Y'all hear that?"

Ishmael recognized the familiar snores of her ex-lover from around the corner of the wraparound porch. She caught herself somewhat wishing that Allen was sitting beside her, lightening the mood.

"Well, it's the perfect time of day for a nap," Maggie said.

"Diane's in the shower. Y'all all good out here on the porch?"

"We're fine, Lena. Couldn't be better. Thank you for getting supper all prepared."

"You know I don't mind. Especially while your grandbaby here."

Lena jerked in the doorway and squealed. Hector appeared behind Lena, smiling.

"Hector Cruz, you better not be messing with my bee-hind! You wanna spanking? I'll show you a spanking! You come here. Come here this instant!"

Hector laughed and dodged Lena's playful swings in his direction.

"Hey, send El Padre down to the dock when he wakes up," he said.

Hector scampered down the steps and across the front lawn toward the dock. Lena huffed and disappeared back into the house, her heavy steps on the staircase audible.

El Padre? Ishmael was stunned. How did Hector know Allen's nickname? Her dad had given Allen that nickname…

Ishmael's eyes grew distant as realizations about her dad flooded her mind. She imagined him—raising his daughter alone with the secret that his wife was both alive and a mermaid, lying to the few friends he had, fabricating stories for the cops after his wife had presumably disappeared.

"Was my dad heartbroken? When she left him?" Ishmael finally asked.

"They both were. Neither of them wanted to be apart," Maggie answered.

"But why didn't we go with her?"

"Your mother wanted you raised on land. Your father stayed with you to carry out your mother's wishes."

"But how could she be so stubborn? I mean, she practically ruined my life."

"Ishmael, Anna wanted you to go to school, learn to speak English. Read and write."

"But, my dad—so he was what, a merman?" Ishmael asked.

"As I've said, I'm not fond of that term. I prefer to use the terms aquatic males and aquatic females," Maggie responded, glancing over the champagne she was about to sip. "Your dad was supposed to tell you everything when you turned eighteen. But then you started dating Allen and—well, things got a bit trickier after that."

Maggie put the glass to her lips and tilted it.

Ishmael was embarrassed. If her grandmother knew about Allen, what else did she know?

"Just because Allen and I—that's no reason to hide stuff from your only daughter! It's absurd! Pisses me off. It was so selfish of him." Ishmael huffed. "So why didn't *you* say anything? You obviously knew my dad took off. You didn't think maybe it was up to you to explain all this to me?"

Maggie shook her head and exhaled. "Sweetheart, I never met you because Richard lost contact with me once your mother was gone. After all, I'm not the easiest person to get in touch with— no phone and all—but he always knew how to reach me—he just didn't. I sent a few letters to him. Never got a response."

"But you said he sent you letters?"

"I said he sent me *one* newspaper clipping. Mind you, the clipping was the only thing in the envelope and there was no return address. He only did it that one time."

Ishmael looked puzzled. "Why would he do that?"

"Clearly, he was proud of you. But I think he didn't want to complicate things. And also, I think Richard was taking your mother's side. I had to respect his decision. It proved to me how much he still loved your mother."

"My mother's side?"

"I told you that your mother and I were . . . not close," Maggie said, standing and walking across the porch to rest her glass on the screen ledge.

Ishmael started to settle down as she detected the genuine anguish in her grandmother's voice.

"What could possibly have driven you and my mother so far apart?"

Maggie sighed, lifting her glass and taking a sip. "We disagreed."

"About what?"

"Everything." Maggie gave her a sad smile. "It was just a million little things. They add up, you know?" Maggie looked back at the unsettled look on Ishmael's face.

"I know it's a vague answer to such an important question. Let's just say that I've put the past behind me. I'm too old to bicker over things that now seem trivial at my age. I've forgiven Anna. I'm just not so sure she's forgiven me." Her eyes grew distant for a bit as she looked off. "Goodness, that's more than enough for now. I'd like to give you some time to process. We'll pick up later where we left off."

"What? No. When? This is my life we're talking about here. My future. I came *across the country*. I've been—"

"I know. And you deserve all the answers I can give you."

Maggie downed the last sip of champagne, pausing in the doorway. "Feel free to make yourself at home. Finish the champagne, if you like."

Ishmael felt the heat rising in her body, a headache coming on. She sighed.

"Dinner will be in about an hour," Maggie added. "Shower. Check out the garden. We've even got a nice coop around back with some happy hens that would probably love to meet you. Especially if you grab a handful of ripe figs off the tree by their pen." She smiled politely. "Help yourself to anything and everything. I'm just delighted to have you here."

Ishmael was left on the porch alone. She leaned forward and rubbed her temples. A hand holding a glass of fizzing liquid appeared in her face. Suddenly the air smelled of Diane's freshly showered skin.

"Here. Drink this, sugar. Makes it all better."

Ishmael looked up. "What is it?"

"An old witch's brew I keep around for times like this." Diane surveyed Ishmael's face. "I'm only kidding, sugar-pie. It's this stuff Captain Harry swears by. He gets it from an Asian market. It'll cure that headache of yours in a snap. Relax your brain. Make you feel like life is easy for a bit."

Ishmael took the glass. She drank the contents in one swig and exhaled. She was left with a bitter taste on her tongue, like she'd just licked the rind of a lemon. She rested her head back on a pillow.

Diane swooped in to retrieve the slender champagne glass off the table.

"Don't mind if I do," she said, pulling the dripping bottle from the ice and refilling the glass. "That Maggie is just the sweetest, prettiest grandmother I have *ever seen*. You're so lucky."

Diane walked over to the screens, setting her glass down and pulling lotion from her pocket.

"Totally. Lucky is the first word that comes to mind," Ishmael said.

"I'm going to ignore that bad attitude and just say that this place is straight out of a movie," Diane said, rubbing her hands together.

Ishmael could smell the lotion. Rose-scented. It smelled nice. Really nice. Maybe that bitter stuff was working. Her headache was diminishing. She watched as Diane sipped her glass like a politician's wife at a lavish party.

"Hey, Ish!" A shout from the dock.

"Damnation. And I know who I'm giving the role of leading male to," Diane said, peering toward the dock.

Hector was waving up to the women on the porch. Diane waved back.

"Diane, do you actually think he can see you batting your eyes from that far away?"

"I'll show you what I'm going to bat if you don't get off this porch! I'm about to call my husband and talk dirty over the phone. I could use some privacy."

Just before Ishmael walked out the screen door, she reached over and took the champagne glass from Diane's hand. She guzzled a hefty swig and was going in for another, but Diane snatched the glass.

Ishmael laughed at Diane's expression. Her laughter was bubblier. Was it the champagne? Or that potion Diane had given her? She was, after all, in her grandmother's house. And the news of her mother . . . Surely that was why she was giddy.

"Ish! Come join me down here!"

She looked toward the dock. Hector was calling her name— her nickname.

"Now, go on. Get!" Diane yelled. "Get off this porch and go talk to that luscious man."

Ishmael pushed the screen door open. "Here goes nothing."

"Nothing, my ripe little ass." Diane grabbed hold of Ishmael's arm and spun her around. "Darling, you have an alternate life as a topless chick with a tail." She hiccupped. "My goodness," she said, looking at her empty glass. "This is good stuff. Wonder where they got this?" She patted her chest with a flutter. "Anywho, sugar, keep your chin up. Being a mermaid has to count for *something*."

15

Hector was smiling as she approached. He took a sip of his beer.

"You don't recognize me, do you?"

"Ah . . ." She looked at him. She did, but she didn't. "Should I?"

"My mom's Maria." He looked for recognition in her face. "We grew up in the trailer park together? I lived three doors down. My name was Jesus back then."

"Wait—Jesus? *Jesus Cruz*?" That's why he'd seemed so familiar to her. "Holy shit."

"So you remember me now?" He grinned.

How could she have forgotten? Jesus Cruz was the best-looking kid that had ever set foot in a trailer park. She probably still had a painting of him somewhere in her trailer—one of the first portraits she ever did.

She flushed.

"Yeah—wow. Great to see you."

He reached in for a hug. It was awkward. She stepped back

and stuffed her hands in her pockets.

"So what's with the new name?"

"Changed my name when we moved to the Bible Belt. Try wearing *Jesus* stitched across a uniform around here." He offered a quick smile. "Hector's my middle name."

"I can't believe you live here," she said. "That's so crazy. I mean, you were—" She took a deep breath. "You were a few years ahead of me, weren't you?"

She'd told Allen that he was her first real crush. And that wasn't totally a lie, was it? She'd fallen for Jesus when she was only twelve. Did that even count?

"Yeah, four years ahead. That's why we never went to the same school. I was in middle school when you were still at Clyde-Elijo Elementary. And then when you went to middle school I was already at Costa Crest High."

"Go Tritons," she said.

"Go Mighty Seahorses. Remember the mascot from middle school?"

He bent down and turned on a green garden hose that hooked up to a makeshift sink. Water trickled out of the faucet, draining into the creek.

"You want to rinse your hand?" He nodded with his chin. "Other one. You leaned against some seagull crap on the railing."

She ran her hand under the water and he offered an edge of his T-shirt for her to dry her hands on. She could smell him: laundry detergent mixed with the sweet but spicy pungency of basil leaves.

"It's good luck," he said.

She looked at him for a moment, puzzled.

"Oh—you mean the bird crap," she said. "Yeah, I think that's only when they're flying over and you get hit."

"Yeah, you might be right."

He sipped his beer. The pause extended into a moment of silence. Hector seemed comfortable in the quiet. A pelican dove in a splash off in the distance, then folded its wings, tucked its bill, and floated on the surface.

"Heard you're a pretty big artist these days," he said.

"I make a living off my paintings, if that counts."

"Counts for me," he said.

She looked around. The main dock connected to the dock house was faded to a dull gray from the sun and salt. A wooden gateway led down a ramp to a narrower floating dock where a trawler was cleated with heavy ropes: a sweeping cast net hung like a massive spider web from the rafters. Faded orange and once-white buoys dangled like oversized Christmas lights from frayed ropes tied to pilings.

"Dried up fish scales." He smiled at her, answering her question, the beer can poised at his lips. "That pile under the filet table. It's fish scales."

It looked like clipped fingernails.

"Stick around and I'll teach you the fastest way to clean a fish."

"It's so strange that you live here," she said, attempting to be subtle about her curiosity. "What a—coincidence."

She smiled. Hector grinned. She could tell that he liked her inquisitiveness, enjoyed stringing her along.

"So how's your mom?" she asked, as he pulled a knife from a holster on the side of the fish-cleaning table and examined it. "Your mom took me shopping for my first bra."

Hector smiled, but he didn't look up from his examination of the knife blade.

"She saved me," she added in his silence. "Otherwise my dad

would have walked me through puberty. Which would have been a disaster."

Hector reached for a sharpening block on the table and started to work on the knife.

"Your dad would've done alright."

"Sure. Who wants to talk tampons with Richard Morgan?"

He looked up from the slick scratching of the metal blade sliding across the sharpening stone. A half-grin appeared on his face as he picked up his beer again.

"Ea-see," he said.

The beer was wedged confidently in his fist. She liked his hands. They looked capable, hard-working. She wondered what they felt like.

"Where is your mom now?" she asked.

He set the beer down and went back to sharpening the knife.

"She lives in Charleston with a fluffy dog. Pretty much moved on and went the complete opposite direction of our life in Cali." He looked over at her and smiled. "It's cool. She was married to my asshole dad for close to twenty years. That's enough to make any woman change course."

Memories suddenly flooded Ishmael. Memories she had long since tucked away. She thought of the times as a kid when she had seen Maria with bruised eyes.

"So that's why you and your mom left the trailer park, isn't it? Because of your dad. I remember that night he got so drunk."

Hector set the sharpening block down and gingerly moved his thumb across the blade, surveying the sharpness. Satisfied, he put the knife back in the holster, then looked up at Ishmael and forced a smile. "Old Joe was drunk pretty much every night." His smile quickly faded to a more serious gaze. "But the night you're talking about, my mom went to the hospital. She was there for a week." Hector looked away. He sipped his beer pensively and paused before adding, "Your dad took charge. Like he always did. Made arrangements for me to stay with a friend in Escondido until Mom got better. I never went back to the trailer park after that night."

"Richard—my dad—took charge? Are you sure we're talking about the same person here?" Her smile vanished when she saw Hector's serious expression.

"Richard locked Ole Joe in a shed until he settled down and sobered up. My dad was a big guy. No one but Richard could have handled him when he was that drunk. Joe's a gorilla."

A memory washed into Ishmael's mind. She remembered how when she was little she had a nickname for Joe. Big Monkey. Joe never could seem to get a coherent sentence out: all he did was grunt.

"But my dad never told me about any of this," she said. For a moment, Ishmael stood in admiration of her dad. He'd stood up to Big Monkey? It seemed impossible.

"You were young. You didn't need to hear about some drunk guy beating up his wife."

Ishmael suddenly realized she was staring. Hector's eyes were . . . she looked away, trying to regain her composure.

"Hey, you want to give me a hand with this motor?" he asked. "Probably not top on your list, but it would sure help to have someone hand me the right tools. You do know what a wrench is, right?"

"I do," she said with a casual clap of her hands, happy to have a task.

They walked down to the lower floating dock. In the afternoon sun, she could see the silhouette of a wind-milling kayak paddle far off down the creek.

Hector reached for a wagon full of tools and pulled it closer.

"Lena's gardening cart," he said, explaining all the hand-painted flowers along the side.

"I'm sure she loves it when you wheel it all the way down to the dock and fill it with greasy tools."

He grinned and crouched down beside the motor.

"Allen seems to be enjoying his adventure up the creek," he said.

"That's Allen?" She held a hand to her forehead and squinted off into the distance. "I thought he was taking a nap."

"He was. Can you hand me a Phillips head?" he asked, opening his hand.

She placed the screwdriver in his hand, and he went to work.

"He woke up and didn't want to bother you and Maggie." He handed the little screws that he was removing to Ishmael. "I rigged him up in the kayak."

Hector pulled his eyes from the motor and grabbed a nearby bucket that he flipped over.

"Have a seat," he said, patting the bucket.

He took a few specific tools from the wagon and put them in Ishmael's lap. As Hector reached for a new screwdriver, his hand grazed her thigh. His forearm muscles glistened in the afternoon heat as he cranked the tool.

"So what ever happened to your dad?" she asked.

"All I know is that he went on a rampage after we skipped town. Nearly beat up your dad trying to get information out of him, about where we'd disappeared to. Richard made us lose contact with him after that."

"I do remember that. You and your mom were there one day, gone the next." She looked out over the water. "Of course, my dad gave me no explanation."

Hector reached over and started taking the small screws from her palm to replace the cover on the motor.

"I don't know for sure, but I think your dad and my mom might have had a little thing going on for a while," he said.

Ishmael shot up. The bucket tipped over behind her. "No way!"

Hector laughed. "Settle down. Don't drop my screws."

He set the bucket back up, and she sat down again.

"That's why your dad sent us here. To Butler Island. To live with Maggie," he explained.

Ishmael sat stunned, frozen in place. Her dad—and *Maria*? But Maria was gorgeous.

Hector noticed the look on her face.

"Aw, you sell your dad short," he said.

He looked off as he turned the screwdriver, smiling. She was enjoying that smile.

"I think that's got it," he said, tightening the last screw. "Let's hope." He yanked the cord, and the motor churned. He nodded, pleased.

"So did anything else ever become of it—between the two of them?"

"Maria's remarried. Right after your dad split and went to South America, she went through this mid-life crisis or something. Everything changed."

Hector wiped his hands on a rag.

"I know the feeling," she muttered.

Hector turned to her. "Oh yeah?"

"So you live in that huge house? With Maggie and Lena?"

Hector started putting his tools away in a metal box.

"I started living in the dock house a few years ago," he said, shifting the tools noisily. "Built the thing myself. Used all scrap wood from the old slave quarters on the property. It took me a few years to complete it," he said, looking up at the dock house. "But I like it. I'm satisfied with my handy-work."

"You built that? I'm impressed."

He put the metal toolbox back in the wagon, offering only a slight smile at the compliment.

"I don't see any cars around here," she said. "Seems odd."

"Well, Detective Morgan, for your information, I work at a boatyard." He raised his eyebrows. "So I drive a boat to work."

"You don't ever want to go anywhere?"

"I can go wherever I want to go in a boat."

"Right." She motioned to the large boat tied up to the dock. "So the big boat is yours too?"

"Bought her from a retired shrimper." Hector stopped organizing his tools to admire the boat. "My goal is to have her fixed up in a year and go live back in some lonely creek." He picked his beer off the railing, drained it, and squeezed the empty can. "Damn, where are my manners?" He looked over at Ishmael. "Lena would tan my hide. You want a beer?"

Hector went inside the dock house, and Ishmael felt a blast of cold air from the open door. A moment later, Hector came out with bottled beers and used the railing and a slap of his fist to pop the tops. He handed one to Ishmael.

"I bring out the glass for my special guests," he said.

They toasted the bottles with a tap and both drank. The corners of his mouth lifted.

"You felt that AC, huh?" he said.

"Pretty steamy around here. Never felt heat like this," she said.

"Get used to sweating day and night. Those old ladies never put in air conditioning." He motioned toward the house with his beer

"I don't think I ever slept straight through a summer night in that house."

Ishmael found herself lingering a little too long when she looked in his direction. His look was refreshingly different from Allen's bohemian surfer image or the starched shirts, monogrammed belts, and pressed pants of Nicholas. Hector looked like a man who could fix things. Hell, he *was* a man who could fix things. He sipped his beer, looking off down the creek. Turning back, he caught her staring and looked her straight in the eyes, continuing to stare even when she looked away.

"I like your hair," he said. "Or—your lack of hair."

Ishmael rubbed her head self-consciously. She kept forgetting that she had shaved her head.

"It suits you. I don't know many women who could pull that off." He pressed the beer bottle to his lips and tilted it back. He looked out over the water, stood up, and jogged down the ramp to the lower dock.

"Beer got a little warm," Hector said, opening the third beer and handing it to Allen. He stabilized the kayak with one hand as Allen climbed out onto the dock.

Allen clicked his bottle against Hector's.

"Beer's a beer, man. Thanks."

They carried the kayak up to the higher dock and turned it upside down. Ishmael realized she was staring at Hector. He moved so fluidly, so relaxed in his own skin.

"Ish, could you believe who this is?" Allen asked. "Never would've guessed a trailer park reunion."

"No joke," Hector said, tapping his beer bottle with the other two. "Ish Morgan and El Padre in the Deep South. Never thought I'd see the day."

"Man, it's been *that long* since that nickname got around?" Allen's face cracked into a cheeky smile. "I must be getting old."

Ishmael sipped her beer, hiding the roll of her eyes.

"Can you dive off this dock?" Allen asked. "I figured I could now since the tide's so high."

"You taking a dip?" Hector was already setting down his beer. "I'll join you. And yeah, dive all you want. Deep-water dock. That's how I'm able to keep the big boat here."

Hector started taking his shirt off and stripped down to a pair of black boxer briefs. Ishmael was sure her jaw dropped at the sight of his body, but she quickly contained herself.

"I figure anything to cool myself off in this heat," Allen said.

"Why don't you join us, Ish?" Hector asked. "Just a quick cool-off before we eat?"

Ishmael was suddenly forced back to her dilemma. What if her body changed in broad daylight?

"Don't have a suit," she said. "We should probably head up. Time for dinner."

"Supper," Hector said. "We call it *supper* around here." He walked down the ramp to the lower dock. "And if you've got on underwear, we won't look too closely when it gets wet," he called over his shoulder. "That is—if you've got on underwear!"

Hector dove off the dock; Allen cannonballed into the water after him. She envied their freedom.

Hector called from the water. "Seriously? I can't persuade you to join us, Ish?"

Allen pulled himself up onto the dock, dripping.

"Man, that felt great," Allen said, reclaiming his beer. He winked at Ishmael. "Promise I won't let him push you in."

"There are towels in a cabinet right outside my front door,"

Hector called from the creek.

Ishmael jumped at the prospect of the chore. "I'll grab them!"

She retrieved the towels and headed back down just in time to catch Hector climbing up the ladder, resembling a Greek god rising from the depths, the glare of the afternoon sunlight on his bare chest. She exhaled and tried to erase her thoughts.

Hector nodded to Allen. "There's an outside shower on the other side of the dock house if you want to rinse off."

"Perfect." Allen took a towel from Ishmael. "See you two up at the house."

Ishmael tossed Hector a towel, but he threw it over the railing.

"Hey, I'm going to swim up the creek a bit," he said. "You want to join me?"

"Ah, you know, I—"

"Heard you could swim as fast as your mom."

There was a suggestion in his voice. Was it possible that he knew about her mother?

"You knew my mom?" she asked.

He gave her a tantalizing smirk. "Come on. I'll race you."

Of course she was tempted. She imagined the two of them swimming down the creek together.

"Naw. I'm really—Rain check?"

"Sure. Okay," he said. He took a step back and she realized how close he'd been standing. "But at some point, I want to see for myself what you got."

He dove off the dock with a perfect splash. She watched him surface a few seconds later; his arms spun evenly, his legs kicked, and his body sliced through the water of the creek.

16

THE REMAINING CANDLES BARELY FLICKERED, having melted low in their glass containers. Allen, Diane, and Hector were drunk, and the conversation had remained light and casual during the meal. Everyone but Ishmael was relaxed. She wasn't sure how she felt about Maggie. Why would a grandmother make no effort to contact her, especially after both her parents had disappeared?

Lena reached over and clicked on a lamp. "Party has come to an end, folks. Getting way too long past my bedtime."

Everyone at the table squinted and moaned at the brightness.

"I'm in charge of cleaning the kitchen," Lena said. "You drunken clowns just take all those empty booze bottles out the house. Recycling bin out by the coop."

There was a sudden scraping of chairs as everyone stood up, clanking the bottles and laughing. Lena lifted the heavy stack of dishes off the table, but Hector reached over and took them from her.

"Well, you're sure good for something," Lena said, following him into the house.

Ishmael started gathering utensils off the table. Maggie put a hand on her shoulder.

"Let them clean up. You and I will finish our wine."

Maggie gestured to the cluster of furniture at the other end of the porch.

"Breeze dropped out. No need to pack us all in that tiny kitchen and sweat ourselves crazy," Maggie said, settling into a chair. "Plus, selfishly, I'll sleep better once I've gotten more of this off my chest."

Ishmael chugged the last of her wine, not sure if she was prepared to hear her grandmother's words. She was drowning in her uncertainties. Could she trust Maggie?

"You *can* trust me, Ishmael. I promise I won't steer you wrong."

Ishmael nearly dropped her glass.

No. No way. It was the alcohol. Too much of it—or perhaps not enough. She spied a wine rack stocked with unopened bottles.

"Those for decoration?" Ishmael asked.

Maggie pulled open a nearby drawer and held up a corkscrew.

"Clean glasses are in the cabinet there by you," Maggie said, twisting the tool into a bottle she had taken from the highest shelf.

"This one is fine."

"Trust me. For this," Maggie said, pulling the cork out with finesse, "you'll want a fresh glass."

"To the ocean," Maggie said, lifting her glass in a toast.

She took a sip and closed her eyes.

Ishmael watched her grandmother, brows raised.

"See for yourself," Maggie said, motioning for Ishmael to take a sip.

Ishmael tasted. A perfect blend of tart and sweet and spice. Plums, rosemary, lavender, raspberries, honey. She held the glass away and peered at it.

"What is this stuff?"

"Special wine for a special time," Maggie said. "It's not every day I get to meet my only granddaughter."

"It's *so good.*"

Ishmael picked up the bottle. There was no label. The glass was fantastically patterned and ornate, like nothing Ishmael had ever seen. It looked like it had been on the bottom of the ocean.

Ishmael looked up. "Where did you get this?"

"Someone's got to drink all the luxuries that go down with the ship."

"But Maggie, this is—"

"Fit for a king?" Maggie sauntered back to her chair, carrying the bottle with her. "I'm sure at one time it truly was. Tonight, it's fit for us queens."

Ishmael hesitated, stupefied by the glass in her hand.

"Come sit down. I still have quite a bit more to tell you."

Ishmael steered her way across the porch and plopped into a chair across from her grandmother.

"Ishmael, the day your truck went off the cliff, you proved something quite remarkable."

Maggie paused and set the wine on the table in front of her. "You were birthed on land; your mother was in the human form when she had you, and you were raised a human child," Maggie continued. "But still, your body seems to have maintained all its instinctual aquatic behaviors."

"But that's what I don't get." Ishmael leaned forward. "I've been in the ocean hundreds of times in my life. My body never changed—but my truck goes plunging off a cliff and my body suddenly transforms? Makes no sense."

"Your body changed to protect you. Instincts kicked in, and your body converted so you would survive."

"So you're saying if my body hadn't changed I would have died when my truck went off the cliff?"

"Most likely. Our aquatic bodies are more resilient to injury."

"But I didn't change until after my car went into the water."

"My thought is that you were already changing before you hit the water; you just didn't recognize the sensation." Maggie shrugged and picked up her wine glass again. "I wish I had more of a precise answer than a theory. We're in uncharted territory here."

Ishmael thought for a while and then looked back toward her grandmother.

"So you're a mermaid too?"

"Of course," Maggie said.

"You say that so plainly."

Maggie laughed. "How am I supposed to say it?"

Ishmael sat back and sipped.

"So why me?" she said. "How did they know to save me when my truck went off that cliff? And how was she there so quickly? How was that female there *immediately* when my truck hit the water?"

"My guess is that she must have sensed it."

"Sensed it. How?"

"How do animals sense a hurricane coming? They don't watch the news. Now granted, a car wreck is not an act of nature, but I still suspect that the female who rescued you must have somehow sensed your truck was going to soar off that cliff."

"You mean—what, like a sixth sense?"

"Somewhat," Maggie said. "It makes me think of my honey bees. If I'm nervous or in a bad mood, they can just sense it. The few times I've been stung are because I went to check my bees with a heavy heart."

"Wait. Hold up." Ishmael held her hands up. "I've had a few glasses of wine. I don't know if I'm ready for all this."

"It's really not that hard to imagine," Maggie said. "Aquatic humans don't have possessions. They have less outward distractions. They're more focused inward. They've cultivated ways to use higher percentages of their brain's potential."

"So they're smarter than us?" Ishmael asked.

"Their focus is just different. Like the ancient yogis. They had such control of their minds that they could do the most astounding things with their physical bodies."

"Sounds smarter to me."

"Yes, in many ways, I agree. But some would argue that living the way they do in the ocean is uncivilized. Certainly, aquatic humans are not 'civilized' in the way that land humans define the word."

Ishmael thought back to that day in the Pacific, the female at the kelp paddy.

Maggie continued. "Most people would say they live like animals—and, strictly speaking, they'd be right. But in many ways, one could also argue that the lives of aquatic humans are possibly more civilized than ours here on land. They don't fight wars. They don't bicker over religion or politics. Their lives in the water are simple. They take only what they need, commune with nature, and—most importantly of all—they don't take things too seriously. Plus, there's plenty of time in the water to play."

Ishmael sat back and sipped her wine. "Sounds nice."

Maggie raised her eyebrows and smiled, apparently pleased that Ishmael was agreeing with her.

The women sat for a moment in contemplation. Maggie leaned

forward to refill the glasses.

"It's just unbelievable to me that the change can happen so quickly," Ishmael said, beginning to relax and open up to her grandmother. "One minute I'm a human, and then seconds later my legs are gone and I have a tail."

"It's not always like that. You're a rarity. Most require a catalyst. Others can't transfer between the species at all."

The sound of a boat's approach stopped both of them. The boat crept by, only its red and green bow lights signaling its presence in the dark water.

"I wouldn't have thought you had neighbors for miles," Ishmael said.

"We don't. That's just Dan. Retired game warden," Maggie said. "He cuts through our creek on low tides. It's faster to get to his son's by boat."

Ishmael looked out over the water, pondering more than the passing boat.

"You don't need a catalyst because you *are* the catalyst," Maggie said. "You're a special breed of aquatic human. By getting in the accident—and your body changing the way it did—you proved this."

Ishmael looked at her. "So I can change back and forth whenever I want to?"

Maggie stood, walked over to the screen, and set her wine down on a ledge.

"I warn you against taking this process lightly." She wouldn't look at Ishmael. "There are some that change and can never change back."

Ishmael jerked upright.

"That's why you're not in the water! You can't go back, can you?"

Maggie turned. Seeing her expression, Ishmael almost wished

he hadn't asked the question.

"You're right," Maggie said. "I can't."

Maggie looked out over the creek. Her flamenco dancing oak trees were silhouetted in the darkness outside, casting dramatic shadows on the blue-black water.

"I was young when I first came to land. I dreamed of a life with cars and refrigerators and movie theaters. I was blind to the risks I was taking."

She looked back at Ishmael.

"Like you, I could change on my own, but I took that ability for granted. Once I converted, that was it for me."

"If you could change once, why couldn't you change again?" Ishmael asked.

"No simple reason. Nothing I could explain." Maggie paused briefly and then added, "Why do women struggle to get pregnant, turn to fertility drugs, have a child, and then get pregnant on their own with the second child?" She looked at Ishmael. "The body shifts. Physiology changes with time."

"Then you must have mated with a human to have my mother?"

"I had a mate from my aquatic life. Not a good match. He hated the land and returned to the water just after I got pregnant."

Maggie looked out of the screen porch with a bittersweet smile.

"Your grandfather was dreadfully handsome, but he wasn't the paternal type."

"So you're stuck?"

Maggie exhaled a thoughtful sigh.

"I don't like to call it stuck. Somehow, my body only came with the hardware to transform once. But I've found a way to enjoy my life here on land."

Ishmael took a deep breath. "That must be so hard for you."

"It was." Maggie came back to sit down in her chair again. "But thankfully, I found Lena. And I love this old house. I don't need much, but what I do need has been provided for me. I give myself credit for at least being wise enough to bring a little stash of gold and jewels when I came to land. I trade them for cash." She laughed. "My one redeeming forethought in my youth—I brought treasure. I came financially prepared."

"So—will I get stuck?" Ishmael asked.

"You've already changed back and forth multiple times now. You seem to have proved yourself highly capable in the process. But there's truly no way to know for sure."

"Great. More ambiguity."

"Transmutation is not exactly a heavily researched process," Maggie explained. "Outside of aquatic mammals, I'm not even sure it exists. I've never heard of another species that can transmutate. Sure, a starfish can grow an arm, a lizard can grow a tail. Humans can clone a sheep. But it's basically our little secret in the ocean. And like any secret, transmutation is mysterious. There are a lot of unanswered questions as to why and how."

Ishmael glanced across the lawn, where a warm apricot glow emanated from the windows of the dock house.

Maggie stood and downed the last of her wine.

"Well, let's plan on talking more tomorrow. We'll take a nice walk. I'll show you around the property."

Ishmael stood quickly. Maggie gave her a confused look.

"Is everything okay?" Maggie asked. "Can I get you something before bed?"

"I just—I don't know—shouldn't I—hug you or something?"

Maggie leaned in and hugged her. She was the same height as Ishmael, and she smelled faintly of lemon balm. Ishmael wrapped her arms around her and hugged her back. Maggie's hair was coarser than Ishmael had expected. Like the mane of a horse. Maggie squeezed her once, tightly, before letting go.

"Well—sweet dreams," Maggie said, and retreated.

Ishmael dropped back into a chair. She rested her head back and exhaled a deep breath. She needed to talk to someone. She thought about waking Allen, but she remembered how drunk he'd been.

She felt something wedged between the cushions of her chair. Diane's cell phone. She pushed a button to check the time, and her eyes squinted in the blue glow. A twinge of a headache cramped her forehead in the brightness. It was almost one in the morning. She exhaled and felt the heat of the wine in her breath. She should go to bed.

But she wasn't tired.

On the West Coast, it was three hours earlier.

On the West Coast, Nicholas was awake.

He had such a *great* voice. And his laugh. It was—perfect. Because Nicholas was fun. So *much* fun. Always up for something spontaneous—last-minute plane flights, breakfast in another city, opening four-hundred dollar bottles of wine at two in the morning.

Yes, Nicholas was fun. He was *great*.

Was this the wine talking? Probably—*not*.

She could just call him. He probably wouldn't answer, but she'd hear his great voice on the greeting. Tell him she was sorry and she was all right. Just—real quick.

She poured herself more wine and took a nice gulp, then sat back and stared at the shiny device until she couldn't take it anymore. Leaning forward, she dialed the number, holding the phone to her ear, breathing and waiting. One ring. Two rings. Holy shit. Her heart pounded. After four rings, his voice came on the line.

"You've reached the voicemail of Nicholas Santorini."

She waited for her heart to swoon.

"I'm with a client or away from my phone. Please feel free to leave a detailed message." *Beep.*

She clicked the phone shut.

She wasn't swooning.

Damnit. Was she crazy? *Yes. Shit!* She didn't want to talk to Nicholas! What would she have said to him? She was an idiot to have called. A drunk idiot. She quickly powered off Diane's cell phone. If Nicholas called back, at least it wouldn't ring. She chugged the remainder of her wine and stumbled into the house. Falling into bed, she pulled the sheets over her body. She wanted to ponder the answers to all her questions, but the wine and fatigue had caught up to her. In no time, she was sound asleep.

17

ISHMAEL AWOKE AT THE DARKEST HOUR, hot and sticky beneath the thin sheet. The ceiling fan whirled overhead, but the night air was still and dank. She rolled to her side. Diane was sound asleep in the next bed, passed out and breathing heavily. In the soft moonlight coming through the windows, Diane's lips were slightly parted, and the dark cherry tendrils of her hair were splayed across the pale pillow.

Ishmael flopped onto her back again and yanked the covers off her legs, hoping to cool off. No wonder: she was still fully dressed. She dragged herself out of bed and searched her bag blindly for something lighter to sleep in. Her thoughts drifted to her grandmother's words about being a special breed of mermaid. What exactly had Maggie meant by that?

Knowing there was no chance of going back to sleep, Ishmael snuck out the front screen door. The night air chilled the sweat on her skin, and goose bumps rose on her arms as her bare feet slid across the dewy grass. She smelled the lurking sweetness of flowers in the yard, their fragrance held static in the breathless air. Without clouds in the sky, there was enough light from the waxing moon to guide her across the lawn. She headed for the dock.

The lights inside Hector's apartment were off, but a floodlight shone down onto the floating dock with a tawny glow. A scattering of moths and beetles swarmed at the incandescence. The insects tapped their hard exoskeleton bodies against the glass of the bulb with an erratic rhythm, their jerky flight the only movement interrupting the stillness of the scene.

Ishmael moved down the ramp toward the floating dock and stood beneath the glow. Spotlighted and barefoot, she was transfixed by the black water before her. She was tempted to jump, but the creek was also eerie, slithering dark below her with a vitreous sheen. The thought of being wrapped in its slippery blackness made her shudder. She couldn't stop thinking about what her grandmother had told her about the risks of transmutation.

She turned to leave, but a premonition stopped her. She suddenly recalled the display on Diane's cell phone. Today's date. This was supposed to be her wedding night.

In another life, she was cutting a cake, dancing her first dance with her new husband. In another life, she was now Mrs. Nicholas Paulo Santorini IV. She thought of herself holding Nicholas's hand, with primped hair, jewelry, makeup, an elaborate dress.

"Ishmael Santorini," she whispered.

Her voice cracked the stillness of the night air. The sound filled her with anguish.

"Look at me," she said to the sky. "What am I doing? Who am I? *What* am I?"

Maybe she should've left Nicholas a message. She'd dialed his number on their *wedding night*. That had to be more than a coincedence

No, that had been *ridiculous*. A drunk dial and a moronic move.

Her brow creased, resisting the urge to cry. Nicholas was a good guy. He would've been a good husband. Surely, they would've been happy. He would've taken care of her. God, she was so confused. She dropped her hands and shook her head. She exhaled heavily and gazed around.

No. *No*. She'd made the right decision. She'd said yes to Nicholas for all the wrong reasons. With Nicholas, she had been sitting on someone else's pot of gold, living out someone else's dream life. She'd been so gutsy that night in Baja. Fearless. Where was that woman now?

She stripped off her clothes, dropped them in a pile on the dock, and dove in. Before she could be afraid, she began to swim, keeping her legs together, using her arms. She felt it: she sensed the wrapping in her lower body, the absorption of one leg into the other, binding them together with a thick skin like scar tissue.

She felt the tugging between her toes. Her lower half lengthened and stretched. There was a slight cramping as her body morphed, but she welcomed the ache. She hovered in the water, undulating her tail underneath her, taking a deep breath, settling into this new form.

She leaned back, lifting her lower half underwater, treading with her hands to keep steady. Her fluke rose above the surface and eased her mind of any doubt or worry. This was the first time she'd truly observed the tip of her own tail. It was dark, but she could certainly tell that her fluke was not the long and flowing tail she had thought a mermaid would have. Instead, it seemed to be some sort of specialized morphing between a porpoise and perhaps a giant bluefin tuna.

It was beautiful. Powerful. Her new strength was liberating.

The water was warm, and Ishmael swam as fast as she could, streamlining her arms at her sides, propelling herself through the water like an arrow shot from a bow. She raced along until a thought slowed her: what, exactly, was possible with this tail? With all this power, could she swim as fast and as skillfully as a porpoise?

She smiled at the thought, kicking hard, thrusting her glorious tail against the water, propelling herself to such a speed that when she surfaced, her entire body was launched out of the water. She soared through the air, feeling the wind on her face, wanting to scream at the excitement that flooded her, the overwhelming exhilaration of flying totally unrestricted, wild and free, through the air.

Her body felt heavy again as gravity caught up with her, and she plunged toward the water, crashing chaotically back into the creek. The skin of her upper body stung from the flop, but without hesitation, she tried the stunt again. And again. And again. Eventually, she was able to gain enough control to breach the surface and lift off into the air, soaring, and then dive back underwater, tucking her head and keeping her arms at her sides, fully beginning to utilize the agility of this new form.

She wasn't sure how long she had moved in one direction down the creek when she instinctively stopped. Glancing around, trying to get her bearings, she saw that the light of her grandmother's dock was only a small shimmer in the distance: it was time to head back. She certainly didn't want to get lost in this darkness. She swam fast underwater, holding her breath, testing her lungs, pushing herself in this new aquatic form, finally surfacing when she could barely discern the hull of Hector's big boat protruding beneath the water.

She rose from underwater, pressing the trapped air from her lungs with a proud, puffing exhale, exhilaration at the realization of what was possible for her. Her bristly scalp crested the surface, and the briny water dripped pleasantly down her face, caressing the creases in her skin and tickling her eyelashes until she actually giggled. She was proud of herself. She lay back on the surface of the creek, suspended in the dark water, bathed in the shine of the floodlight.

Her buoyant body held itself effortlessly afloat; she gratefully tasted the salt on her lips. She looked up at the stars, trying to take in the magnitude of all that was happening to her. Her breath was heavy from the swim, but she was giddy with excitement. Finally, she closed her eyes, savoring the moment, and drifted into a blissful meditation, feeling as weightless as if she were levitating.

Her eyes sprung open. She'd heard a noise. She looked to the dock and saw a figure perched in the darkness.

It was Hector, and he was looking right at her.

Ishmael was dizzy with the sight of him. His silhouette was only partially illuminated by the glow of the floodlight, his sable hair loosened messily from what had been a ponytail. His shirt was off, and he sat on the ramp that led down from the dock to the floating one. He rested his forearms on his thighs and leaned into them. His rippled torso curved beneath his strapping shoulders, producing in Ishmael thoughts of wrapping her arms around him, pulling him in close. They were alone, and the night and the water only increased the intimacy of the moment.

"What—you doing?" he asked. His voice sounded strange.

"Ah—I was hot," she said. This was no time to be caught off guard. She looked around. Had he seen her? All of her? "I decided to take a swim," she added, attempting to sound calm.

"AC at my place. You should've come." He paused and swayed ever so slightly before adding, "I thought you'd come."

Ishmael hovered in the water. Normally she would've been quick to respond, but she had a fluke for feet and that fact panicked her. Hector continued in her silence.

"I was hoping—you'd come—to my place. After your little chat—with Maggie—on the porch."

He was still drunk.

"Hey—when did you get here?' Ishmael said, wondering if he had seen any of her tricks down the creek.

"Long enough."

Hector stood. The sticky night air, combined with the gleam of the dock light, made his skin glow with sweat. He tripped on Ishmael's pile of clothes on the dock and kicked. The clothes scattered. He spun, imbalanced by the sudden movement.

Ishmael hovered low and pretended to use her arms to tread water. It was dark except for the one dock light: maybe he hadn't seen her turning flips down the creek. Maybe he hadn't seen her tail. Damn, she hoped not.

"You stole my idea," Hector said. "*I* go for swims when I can't sleep."

Ishmael wasn't sure what to do. Her clothes were on the dock at Hector's feet, and the only way she knew to get rid of this body was to let her skin dry out. *Shit.* She hadn't thought this through.

Hector walked over to a piling and snagged a bottle. When he turned into the light, Ishmael saw that he was taking a swig from a near-empty handle of whisky.

"That was—" He hiccuped. "Quite a show." He glared at Ishmael, and she noticed for the first time how bloodshot his eyes were, how vacant. Hector wasn't drunk—he was wasted.

"Tell me how long you've been standing there."

"Long—*enough*." He hiccupped again. Hector's voice was garbled, his eyes half shut. "So is this what you and Maggie—had the little chat about?"

"What little chat?" Ishmael stalled, looking desperately around for a way out. "About what?"

Hector pointed at her with the near-empty bottle, and what was left of the whisky sloshed inside.

"*The* chat. The one about—" He swayed and accentuated his next words with emphatic jerks of the bottle. "A-bout you being a mermaid."

"I—ah—I'm not sure—" she stuttered. *Shoot.*

"My dad—" He lifted a sluggish finger. "Did you know—ole Joe couldn't even *talk*?" He paused, looked around, and then came back to life. "That asshole—typed stuff on my mom's arm." He mimicked typing with his fingers, still clutching the bottle in one hand. He laughed. "Freaking mermaid Morse code."

Ishmael tried to think back to the trailer park, to remember Joe and Maria, to comprehend what Hector was saying.

"Your parents—they did it. Hell, they changed. Just like *that*!" He tried to make his fingers snap in connection with his words but couldn't muster the coordination, remaining mesmerized by his fingers for a stint. "It was our family," he said, finally looking up, "we got the shit end of the stick. We got *trapped*!" He spit the last word and lifted an arm to wipe the drool with the back of his hand.

"Hector—I'm not sure what you're talking about. Let's—ah—"

"Fuck you, Ishh-male." The words sloshed from his mouth. He looked straight at her, eyes burning. As he stood in the light, she could see he was sweating profusely—his moist hair clung to his neck and face.

"Look, I'm sorry—"

"FUCK YYOOU!" He tilted his head back and shouted the words to the sky.

Hector threw the bottle against a piling, and the glass shattered. Ishmael was far enough away, but she covered her face with her hand; when she looked up, shards of the bottle covered the dock.

Hector turned and pressed one hand into a railing to steady himself. His hand slipped on the railing, and his knees bent underneath him, collapsing his legs. Only his armpit, wedged awkwardly atop the railing, caught him from falling into a heap.

He looked around, dazed. The jolt of the fall had awakened him briefly. His eyes were wide for a moment, staring blankly, but then his head rolled sloppily again on his neck. Ishmael could see his face in the light of the dock. He looked like a totally different person than the handsome guy she had talked to that afternoon.

He looked exactly like his dad.

Ishmael cringed at the sight.

"Turn off!" he yelled. Hector grabbed the air for something. He looked at the light and cursed. Ishmael realized he was trying to somehow reach for a switch to turn the dock light off.

"I left—the light on for yooou—Ish-may-elle." He pronounced her name in a sing-song voice and said the words without looking at her. "Left the light on—for you—Ish-may-elle-Mor-gan. Left it onnnn—so you'd come down here—swimmy-swimmy."

He pushed off the railing, muttering curses, and started to make his way off the dock. He didn't look in Ishmael's direction, as if he had forgotten she was even there. Ishmael swam closer, knowing she needed to be alert in case he decided to return. The dock was covered in glass. She looked up at Hector's trawler. The boat towered high above her. Perhaps she could use her tail to launch herself up onto the deck. She had to get rid of this tail.

She kicked with her tail and sprung futilely upward toward the deck of the boat. Her wet fingers slipped from the slick surface, and she fell back into the water with a loud plunge.

Before she could even hesitate and doubt herself, she kicked forcefully again, thrusting herself out of the water. Her hipbone smacked against the hull. She pulled her heavy tail up onto the deck of the boat with the adrenaline-pumping strength of her arms, breathing heavily. Her body was dripping, and she lay on the deck, looking up at the stars.

There was a loud splash.

She glanced around, listening, holding her breath. She heard nothing else and rested her head back onto the deck.

Wait. Had Hector fallen?

Rolling onto her stomach, her heavy tail flipping like a massive rubber pancake behind her, she peered through a slit in the railing of the boat. She could barely see in the darkness, but she was sure that Hector was no longer on the dock. Believing and not believing, she examined the water for any sign—a bubble, a ripple. He wasn't swimming or even thrashing in the water. He must have tripped. Hit his head. Knocked himself out and then fallen in the creek. Hector was drowning.

Shit. Her legs had begun to separate, but they were still glued with gummy straps of skin. Her feet were wedged together, bound at the heels so that they stuck out like a ballerina in first position, her toes flattened like coins left on a train track. She dragged her useless lower half across the deck, moving her torso with all the strength she could muster from her exhausted arms. Finally, she reached the stern of the boat and lugged her heavy, deadweight lower half up onto the transom.

She glanced down. Yikes. Long way down. She closed her eyes and plunged headfirst back into the water. In the air she flipped, and her weighted, inept legs struck the water first. Her thick-skinned lower half sunk her immediately, dragging her downward. She struggled to the surface, unable to kick with legs or to thrust with a tail, and she paddled awkwardly over to where she had heard the plunge, choking on her own splashing, barely keeping her head above water. She prayed her body would change back so she could have more control.

At first she could see nothing in the black water, but then she noticed a ripple on the surface. Could it be?

She felt the change, thankfully, and sensed the wrapping of her lower half, the thick skin like rubber binding her legs together. She kicked and felt the power of her fluke. She took a deep breath, and then dove. The underwater was like ink, but she felt with her hands, searching wildly, contorting her tail to maneuver her body in all directions, to cover the complete area.

She came up for a breath and dove once again.

Hector had said that afternoon that this was a deep-water creek. She was beginning to see the truth of those words. She thought back to the afternoon. Hector had been a different person then. She'd fallen for him. Now those feelings embarrassed her. He disgusted her—but she certainly couldn't let him die.

She dove again, searched, and came up gasping for air. She forced her mind to calm—talking to herself—willing herself to focus, not to lose it. She dove again. Her fingers were spread wide underwater, reaching out blindly. Nothing. She felt only the soft, gooey mud of the bottom. She came up for one more gulp of air and again dove quickly. Her heart pounded in her chest from the quick breaths, the diving, and the fear. She scoured the muddy floor with her hands again, her cheeks puffed full of air, her eyes open wide but worthless in the inky water.

Then her fingertips grazed something. Clothing. She grasped the waistband of his pants with one hand and strongly tugged it toward her. She felt the heaviness of Hector's body. She wrapped an arm around his neck and kicked her tail, racing to the surface.

She used her tail to hover and hold him in her arms, floating his body on the surface. Hector was muscular but slender. Medium frame. She could do this, couldn't she? She was strong. Her tail was powerful in this form. She had to at least try.

She swam fast and thrashed her fluke, propelling Hector's body and her own toward the dock with a loud crash. She held on to him with one hand and wedged her fingers into the gap between the slats of two boards. Her forearms flexed with the strain. At least for a moment, this grasp was holding the both of them. It gave her a second to think. Her arms ached, but she wasn't losing ground. She lifted her tail and tried to use her fluke to work a leg of Hector's up onto the dock.

Her fingers slipped.

She kicked repeatedly, pulling Hector's body slowly onto the dock with determination. Her chest heaved. She tasted the tears on her face, slightly sweeter than the salty water of the creek.

His legs were as heavy as her tail. Why were they so heavy? The glass from the broken whisky bottle crunched beneath them, but she barely felt it. Finally, she had gained enough ground. She held onto the waistband of Hector's pants as she positioned her own body securely on the dock. She sat up, her rigid tail cantilevering out over the edge of the dock, useless when out of the water. One final grunting yank and she pulled his body fully onto the dock.

She lay back, crying, breathless.

She flipped his body over and checked to see if Hector was breathing. He wasn't. She called his name, slapped his face. No response. She clamped his nose with her fingers and breathed twice into his mouth. His tongue was the husky taste of whisky, and his bluish lips were the bitter taste of brine. She breathed into him again. Nothing.

She started chest compressions. "One, Two, Three, Four, Five." She counted out loud to keep herself sane. *Was he dead?* Her own breath pounded in her chest. She pinched his nose and breathed again. Chest compressions. Close off the nose again and puff-puff into his mouth. Chest compressions. "One, Two, Three, Four, Five!" Close off the nose. *Shit. What's happening?*

He sputtered. Water flowed from his mouth, and he coughed, raspy and congested. His eyes opened. The round ocular spheres spun in their sockets without recognition and then rolled back into his head. His heavy lids slowly lowered.

Ishmael put an ear to his sternum and heard a heartbeat; she felt his chest rise once and then fall. He was breathing. She checked the pulse in his wrist. Her hands trembled. She put her face near his and felt the warmth of his liquor breath. He was alive.

She sat back and stared at the body. She'd never been that scared. She'd been less scared when her truck went off the freaking cliff.

She looked down and saw that without her awareness her lower half had transformed back to legs. Her toes were still slightly webbed, but she pushed herself up to standing regardless. Only a few trickles of blood drizzled on her bare skin from the broken glass. Her clothes, scattered on the dock, were sopping wet. She yanked the wet shirt over her head, and then jerked on her shorts.

Tip-toeing across the floating dock, careful of the glass beneath her feet, she reached the main dock and ran to the dock house.

She found a broom and hurried back down the dock, waddling in a pair of Hector's rubber boots, carrying a broom over her shoulder. Hector never stirred, even when she moved him aside to sweep beneath his body. She knew she was going to have to get him off the dock. She couldn't carry him, but could she possibly drag him?

No. Wait. She remembered Lena's gardening cart. Of course. She pulled the flower-painted wagon from the corner of the dock and removed the metal box of tools. She shifted Hector's legs first and then grasped beneath his armpits to hoist his upper body onto the cart. It was clumsy; Hector's legs overflowed, but the wagon at least held the bulk of his body. It was a rising tide so the ramp wasn't as steep up to the main dock. She wedged his arms tightly across his chest, and hauled the cart slowly through the gateway and off the main dock. She parked the wagon just outside the dock house door, panting, and paused. He was in a safe location. He was alive. She'd done her part.

But could she just leave him there? Splayed out in the cart like that?

Yes. He was a jerk.

She caught her breath. She couldn't leave him there. She turned the knob on the dock house door and felt along the inside walls, flipping on a light.

Ishmael froze. She wasn't sure what she'd expected to find, but certainly not this. An enormous world map spanned one entire wall, covered with tiny red pushpins marking positions in oceans all over the world. Newspaper clippings were strewn about. Technical-looking charts were stacked in chaotic piles. Books collected in messy stacks throughout the room, bright tabs jutting wildly from their pages as placeholders. Exotic shells and feathers littered the windowsills. The room looked like the office of some absent-minded oceanography professor.

Hector mumbled outside: she yanked the wagon inside, stopped the cart beside his bed, and grabbed him beneath the armpits. In one last heaving effort, she managed to sling Hector's shoulders onto his bed and maneuver the rest of his body onto the mattress. His pants were soaked. Should she take them off?

Nope.

She watched him for a moment, checking his breathing, then switched the light off and closed the door. She slid off the clumsy white boots and darted across the lawn. Peeling the creaky screen door open just enough for her body to slip through, she silently crept into the house, stripped off her damp clothing, put on a dry T-shirt, and slid into bed. She held her breath as she positioned herself under the covers, making sure Diane hadn't stirred. Lying completely still, eyes wide open, she listened.

Nothing. Her body loosened.

What a night. Her mind was still racing. What had Hector been talking about on the dock? What did he mean when he said his family was "trapped?"

She clamped her eyes shut—she had to get some rest, and dawn was fast approaching. She wasn't ready for the sun to rise yet, but in the daylight, things would be clearer and she'd have more perspective.

She took ten deep breaths, slowly, counting them, forcing a calm over her exhausted body. The humming of the fan, combined with Diane's soft breathing, soon triumphed over the chattering in her head and lulled her into a heavy sleep.

18

IN THE MID-MORNING LIGHT, she dug through her box of art supplies. Drawing would ease her mind. Hunting for a sharpener, she nudged the bed and felt for the first time the ache in her upper thigh. She pulled her nightshirt up and looked down. A massive yellowish-purple bruise was forming on her hip from the night before.

What a night.

She was not looking forward to seeing Hector. Such a waste. He was an attractive guy. Wait. No. *Gross.* She couldn't believe she was still thinking like that. I mean, sure, she could appreciate his strong back. The flowing black hair wasn't so bad either. And those eyes. Like hunks of obsidian . . .

"How'd you sleep?"

Ishmael spun around. Shoot. Had she been talking out loud?

Maggie was standing in the doorway. Her straw hat hung against her back from a leather cord around her neck. The room around her was a disaster of clothes and shoes and toiletries. Mostly Diane's mess, but Ishmael was embarrassed.

"How about that walk I promised you last night?" Maggie asked.

Ishmael set down the pencils in her hand.

"Maggie, I'm sorry if I was rude last night. I—I'm not really feeling like myself and—I came all this way to see you, and I feel like—"

"Well, I'll take that as a yes. I won't take no for an answer anyway. We're going to pick blackberries. There's a wild thicket that's looking ripe just up the road on our property." Maggie tripped over some clothes on the way out, without commenting or even turning around. "I'll be waiting out back."

Ishmael splashed cold water on her face and threw on some shorts and a clean T-shirt. Her outfit didn't match, as her options were slim, but she hardly cared. She found her grandmother sitting on the back steps. Maggie didn't turn around when the screen door slammed. Her hair was pulled back exactly as the day before. Silver wisps escaped the braid, giving the arrangement an indelicate and purposeful look.

"I hope you won't be too hot," Maggie said. "It's a steamy one today."

Maggie stood and started walking down the road.

"No shoes?" Ishmael asked.

Maggie turned briefly, "I wear them only if I have to."

Ishmael smacked her arm, leaving a bloody smudge.

"You've got to be *one* with the mosquito," Maggie called over her shoulder. "Like a beekeeper is one with the bees."

Ishmael hurried down the steps and caught up with her grandmother.

"That's quite an outfit you've got on there," Maggie said. "I didn't realize tie-dye had made its way back in style. You and Allen seem to be sure of it."

Ishmael, who had barely slept the night before, was too tired to be offended. As they moved farther away from the creek along the dirt road, the breeze completely died. She hadn't anticipated the heat would be this intense. She wiped her sweaty upper lip with the inside collar of her T-shirt: it was Allen's shirt, and it smelled faintly of incense. A wave of hangover hit her.

"What's the matter—can't keep up with an old lady?"

"If you tell me my grandfather is Poseidon, I'm turning around."

"I'm not making this stuff up," Maggie said, shrugging her shoulders. "Remember what I told you last night? That you're a special breed of aquatic human?"

Ishmael nodded. "Of course. That's why I couldn't sleep."

"In your aquatic form, you're an alpha female," Maggie said. "That's your ticket. You don't need an outside catalyst to move between your aquatic form and your human form."

Maggie stopped and perked up.

"Hear that? Car just turned onto our road."

She looked off at the tree line in the distance. A grind of shifting gears exposed the culprit of the dust cloud.

"Must be Leon. He really can't drive straight-stick for diddly-squat."

Ishmael started walking again. She rubbed her head in an attempt to stop the pounding.

"Are you alright?" Maggie asked.

"No. I'm hung over." She kept her hands on her head but looked at her grandmother. "So how does it work exactly?"

"It has to do with pheromones. And I'm sorry to say that this is as close to an answer as I can give you."

"That's it?" She looked over at her grandmother. "Pardon my French, Maggie, but that's bullshit."

"The only human example that might compare is how women who are together somehow start to share the same menstrual cycle. It's one female, the alpha, that usually dominates and therefore sets the cycle. In our case, the alpha female somehow sets the stage—makes it possible—for the process of transmutation to occur."

"I still don't understand why you were able to change once and then weren't able to change back," Ishmael said.

"Oh, who knows? The alignment of the planets? The barometric pressure? Chakras not properly tuned?" She lifted her arms up to the sky. "Transmutation is nothing if not a mystifying process."

Maggie caught Ishmael's eyes.

"You want answers, I know. Clear-cut, rational, precise. I was that way once. But that's not how this works. The more we find out about this universe we live in—the cosmos, the atomic particles, the energy that forms matter—the more we realize how little we really know."

Ishmael stared blankly at her grandmother.

"Okay, granddaughter—well, let's see here. Let me tell you something that might appease you. How about this? You come from the strongest lineage of alpha females. It was my great grand-mother who discovered this whole transmutation process. There's a nice fact for you to chew on."

Maggie started walking again. Ishmael hastened to catch up.

"So you're an alpha too?" Ishmael asked.

"I am. Though not as powerful as you, which I've proven simply by the fact that I changed forms once and was not able to change back."

Maggie kept a brisk pace. Ishmael's head was spinning with information; she struggled to think and walk.

"You're more like your mother," Maggie explained. "Strong. Courageous."

"I'm like her?" Ishmael felt pride, but the feeling was quickly overcome by a tinge of resentment. "Guess I'm not quite sure that's a good thing."

"Your mother—well, her *alphaness*, for lack of a better word— was just exaggerated somehow. She could transmutate faster than anyone our kind had ever seen." Maggie stopped briefly, tilting her head to look at Ishmael with raised eyebrows. "That is, until you came along."

A rusted red pickup was now barely visible at the end of the road. The sight caught Maggie's attention, and she paused to watch the approaching truck.

"Lena must be going shopping in town today," Maggie said.

Ishmael stood beside Maggie, deep in thought. Finally, she asked. "So what does that mean—her *alphaness* is exaggerated?"

Maggie pulled her eyes away from the truck. "Well, it means your mother's pheromones are stronger, so the process works faster and cleaner with her. It means that if Joe and Maria Cruz had come to land with your mom, they probably wouldn't have had any problems."

Ishmael's eyes glazed over, transfixed by her sudden realization. "Maria and Joe were . . . wait a minute, you mean Hector—"

"Is from an aquatic bloodline, yes. Like you."

The truck pulled up next to them.

The driver was a massive man with skin that glistened like a polished coffee bean. He wore overalls, and the forearm that hung out the window was as thick as a hefty tree branch.

He tipped his hat.

"Maggie." His voice was so deep it was barely intelligible.

He turned to acknowledge Ishmael with a slight nod of his sturdy chin.

"Well, hello there, Leon," Maggie said in a cheerful voice, taking a different tone than she had been using with Ishmael. She pulled her straw hat from off her head, and it hung down her back from the leather cord. "Mighty kind of you to take Lena into town. This is my granddaughter, by the way, Leon."

Leon tipped his hat again. His eyes shifted up the road to the house. Maggie had her hand resting on the side mirror, and she turned around and looked over her shoulder. Lena stood on the back steps.

Maggie tapped the truck twice with her hand.

"Always good to see you, Leon."

Maggie stepped back, and the rusty truck rolled along toward the house.

"You told him who I was," Ishmael said as he pulled away.

"I didn't tell him your name." Maggie looked at Ishmael. "Oh, don't get all fussy. He's not exactly the town gossip."

Maggie veered off into the brush on the side of the road and reappeared, dusting off two buckets she had retrieved.

"We've got a little shed tucked back up in those trees," Maggie explained with a smile as she handed a bucket to Ishmael. "I got these big ones for all the blackberries we're going to pick."

Maggie and Ishmael could hear the truck approaching behind them; Lena was hanging her head out the passenger side, talking loudly over the growl of the diesel motor.

"We'll drive slow this time up the road. That dust cloud nearly *choke* y'all the first time!"

Leon stopped the truck. His deep voice grumbled as much as the truck's engine.

"Gettin' us some rain thus afa-noon," he said, looking off as if he could already see the rain clouds coming. "That help the dust."

"I'll keep an eye out for rain clouds. Thank you, Leon." Maggie said. "Make sure we don't get caught in a downpour."

"Ishmael," Lena beckoned, "You look pale as a ghost. You feeling sick, child? Y'all hop in this truck and we'll drive y'all to them berries."

Ishmael was tempted, but Maggie responded for them.

"Oh, we'll be fine. My granddaughter can handle it." She poked Ishmael in the ribs. "Leon, I've been meaning to tell you, that okra you gave us last week was the best I've ever had. You seem to pick it just right at the perfect time."

"Yessum. Thank ya."

Lena walked around to the back of the truck holding a basket, and Ishmael noticed that Lena was wearing hot-pink flip-flops with her apron. The apron strings hung loose about her waist.

"I packed y'all a thermos of lemonade. Few of my homemade sweet buns in there, too."

Maggie smiled. "What would we do without you?"

"Oh, you'd survive," Lena said, hiking her dress as she climbed into the truck. "Mm-hm. I do like some berry pie. Get us those real juicy ones."

The truck eased away. Maggie smirked.

"I haven't told anyone this, but I think Lena has a crush on old Leon. Just you watch. When she comes back from a day with him, she'll be as chatty as a cheerleader."

Maggie pointed off down the road.

"The thicket's just a little-ways up the road. There's a nice big oak tree there. We can have a seat in the shade and sweeten you up with one of Lena's cinnamon rolls. But let's get a move on.

If Leon says it's going to rain, it's going to rain."

Maggie adjusted her straw hat on her head and marched forward.

"So I'm having a little trouble here," Ishmael said. "Swallowing the fact that Hector is—well, like me."

"Hector was born on land like you, but he's never been able to change." Maggie said. "Which isn't that strange considering both his parents couldn't change back."

"This is ridiculous. Why were all these aquatic parents coming to land if there was such a risk?"

"Good question. I've pondered this exodus many times. Bottom line, they all were searching for the best future for their kids."

"So Hector's never—?"

Maggie looked at Ishmael. "Even in your mother's presence and mine together, the alpha energy wasn't strong enough. Just because I can't change anymore doesn't mean I've lost my alpha-ness—it just means I've used up the trick on myself, I guess. But it didn't work on Hector." She looked forward, growing pensive. "Or maybe something else was missing . . . something we don't understand yet. It crushed Hector at first," she said, shaking her head. "But he's beginning to accept his fate."

"Joe Cruz—no wonder he was such a drunk. He was trapped on land."

"Exactly. And males have a harder time facing that fact, I've discovered. What made it worse for Joe was that he never really learned to talk when he came to land. On top of everything else, he couldn't properly communicate like a human."

Ishmael walked slower for a moment, pondering.

"Okay, this all makes more sense now. The female that saved me—she didn't speak. For some reason, I guess I just figured that mermaids—since they look so similar to us in the face and all—would talk."

"Opening the mouth underwater to voice something would be absurd, so in the ocean, aquatic humans don't use speech like we do on land. They communicate in other ways."

"So you couldn't talk when you first came to land?"

Maggie shook her head.

"Wow. What did you do?"

"Like learning any language, I took my time. The ability to talk is vestigial in aquatic humans. The capacity is dormant, but using the voice box for speech is still accessible. When aquatic humans come to land, they simply have to work at it and they can learn. At least, most of them can. Hector's father was an exception."

Maggie pulled a white handkerchief from a pocket in her pants and wiped her forehead. She pointed off to the side of the road. "The blackberry thicket is in that small clearing. Let's sit in the shade for a bit and have a little snack before we get to picking."

The oak's branches draped all the way to the ground and swooped at one place into a perfect little bench. Both women took a seat, and Maggie removed her straw hat. Ishmael poured lemonade into the lid of the thermos.

"I always thought Joe just didn't talk," Ishmael said. "I didn't know he *couldn't*."

"Do you recall that Joe used to type on Maria's arm when he wanted to communicate?"

Ishmael nodded, remembering. So that was what Hector was talking about last night on the dock.

Maggie continued. "Well, that's an older form of communication in the water. It's becoming a bit outdated. Typing-on-the-arm is comparable these days to sending a fax versus sending an email. The younger ones really are so savvy with their mental capabilities nowadays. They communicate more with subtle sounds and minor telepathy."

Ishmael looked at her grandmother as though she had just arrived from another planet.

"Telepathy."

"I've mentioned it before," Maggie said. "Don't be so shocked."

"Oh, I'm beyond the shock phase." Ishmael thought back to the day when Allen and Diane dropped her off in the boat. "The female in the water—in the Pacific—she was trying to communicate with me that way. She kept grabbing my arm. It freaked me out."

Ishmael smacked another mosquito on her arm. "Am I the only one getting bitten here?"

Maggie retrieved a small box and matches from her pocket.

"Citronella incense," she said. "This'll keep the bugs at bay."

Pungent smoke wafted through the air around them.

"So do you know which one I'm talking about?" Ishmael asked. "The female who brought my ring back?"

"Heavens no. The ocean is huge. But word travels fast. I caught wind of the news that your ring had been returned to you. And I had a feeling you'd know what to do with it."

"So the plan all along was for me to pawn my wedding ring?"

"I wouldn't say *plan*, but I did know you'd need some money after what you'd been through. And I was hoping you wouldn't go back to Nicholas for it."

"So you know about Nicholas too?"

Maggie shifted the stick of incense until the smoke wafted more in their direction.

"Mainly, I was just happy to hear you were back in the water so quickly after your swim home from Baja . . . To know you were craving the water and that you weren't afraid of your aquatic form."

"So what, they have a mermaid broadcast or something? How do you know all this?"

"In a sense. Aquatic humans, though global, are a small community. We stay connected. Remember, while humans on land are separated by water, aquatic humans are connected by it. News travels fast when it's uninterrupted."

"Then how come you don't know where my mom is?"

"Because your mother doesn't like to be found. As I've mentioned, she's skillful. Pretty much travels alone. Keeps herself off the radar, so to speak. She likes it that way."

Ishmael thought for a moment. "Well, she can't possibly avoid all of them?"

"Oh, she makes contact. That's how I know she's alive. There are now enough of us ex-aquatics on the land that she can spread word when she wants to."

"Enough. How many is enough?"

"Couple of hundred."

Ishmael pondered this for a moment. "So she contacts ex-aquatics? What? She just swims up to them?"

"Perhaps. If the time is right and safe. But more than likely, she leaves a token for them somehow. A unique shell left on the steering column of a boat. An elaborate knot tied in an anchor line. A bottle of deep-sea port left mysteriously on a dock. Pretty much every ex-aquatic still has some contact with the ocean. We're around the water enough, and we know what to look for."

Maggie put her hand on Ishmael's. "Look, I know you want to find her. And I'll do everything I can to help. I've sent word out that you're here. I have a hunch she'll turn up."

Ishmael's heart thundered in her chest. *Her mother might turn up?* She felt her grandmother's soft hand slide off her own.

Maggie took a deep breath.

"I want you to know that the numbers of aquatic humans are dwindling in the ocean. There were several thousand at one time. Now there are probably just under a thousand. At least air travel is more prevalent these days—no more small boats slowly crossing the oceans with watchmen, so it's a bit easier for them to stay hidden. Nowadays, the boats are so computerized, they miss catching a glimpse of an aquatic human fluke on the horizon."

"Where do they live?"

"Areas where humans on land mainly keep to themselves and respect the ocean. Coastal Oregon. Baja. Bermuda. Finland. There's a small pod off the coast of Scotland. Nova Scotia. Nicaragua. They find sea caves. Or sleep wrapped in kelp beds for protection. There are all sorts of ways to survive out there when you are adapted to live in the water."

Ishmael winced, remembering her day in the Pacific: the massive beast she'd seen in the water that day. "What about sharks?"

"I was waiting for that question. Humans are so fascinated by sharks." She looked at Ishmael. "The fact is aquatic humans are simply smarter than them. Sharks aren't stupid, don't get me wrong, but they're less of a threat than you'd think. Maybe they just don't like the way we taste."

Maggie laughed.

"Co-existence is a wondrous thing. Thankfully, aquatic humans have incredible adaptations and instincts to protect them. As I've mentioned, they are really more animal than human, connected to nature in a way land-dwelling humans have mostly lost."

"The female was so awkward that day in the Pacific. I was expecting her to be more human," Ishmael said. "She just—she looked human from the waist up."

"When I first came to land," Maggie said, "I was basically as feral as a wild animal in comparison to now. I blended in by using gestures, pretending I was very shy. In the water, there are the subtlest meanings in gestures and sensations. Squeaks, squeals, grunts, chirps—they all have their significance. I kept the gestures when I first got to land, but I quickly learned to suppress the urge to squeak or grunt—I noticed right away how strange those noises were to humans. People generally like animals with human character-istics; they don't like humans with animal characteristics."

Ishmael thought of Joe Cruz. The pieces of the puzzle were coming together now.

"So my grandfather came to land with you. Since you were an alpha female. You were his ticket to conversion."

"Transmutation, yes. There were quite a few of us back then, plenty to choose from. He could have found another alpha female to bring him to land. And he eventually did, the bastard."

Maggie fanned herself with her hat.

"Oh, he would have *loved* you," Maggie said. "He could just sniff out the most powerful of the alpha females, and those were the ones he wanted to tame."

Ishmael waited for her to continue. She was riveted.

"It boggles the mind to think of it," Maggie said. "How strong you are. Leads me to believe that this alpha gene is somehow growing more powerful with each generation."

Ishmael poured more lemonade into the lid of the thermos. "I want to hear more about the bastard."

"Grab a bucket. I'll tell you while we pick."

Ishmael chugged the cool liquid and followed her grandmother past the pine tree. Maggie went right to work, plucking a berry and sliding it in her mouth, chewing for a moment as she thought.

"I got pregnant that first night we slept together on the beach. We were both so elated that night, beneath the moon, in our new human forms. Having legs for the first time. Feeling dry sand between our toes. I guess the excitement spread to our loins."

"I'm not sure I want to hear—"

"Oh, we were so young! Driftwood hutch. We had the beach all to ourselves. It was blissful. But then one night, your grandfather wanted to change back. I was pregnant, so I told him I wouldn't. But your grandfather, he was nothing if not persuasive."

Maggie dropped another handful of berries in her bucket.

"Watch for the thorns," Maggie said, popping a few more berries in her mouth. Her lips were just starting to show stains from the juice. "They make these berry bushes now—somehow genetically they do—and they are *thornless*. Can you imagine that? These are wild. And that means plenty of thorns. They're juicier to me, so they're worth a few scratches."

Ishmael watched her grandmother's trained hands. Her own hands were already scratched with thin crimson lines.

"As you know," Maggie said, "I discovered my predicament that night. Turned out that was only to be the first of many let-downs of the evening." Maggie shook her head and sighed again.

"Why? What else happened?" Ishmael asked.

"Another female showed up. He'd been cheating on me all along. The look I saw pass between her and your grandfather . . ." She looked at Ishmael with a matter-of-fact smile. "But I'm not even sure he was in love with either of us. I think your grandfather just loved the accomplishment of wooing an alpha female."

"What an asshole."

"Yeah. He was. But he got what he deserved. He tried to come to land again, and the transmutation didn't go through one hundred percent. Something went wrong. Poor bastard was stuck with only half a fluke—not that I really feel sorry for him. Anyways, they say he died in a storm. He wasn't able to swim with his deformed tail."

"So, wait a minute—there can be side effects from the transmutation process?"

"This is anatomical transmutation we're discussing here, not brushing your teeth. Things can go wrong."

"But—I'm fine, right? I don't have anything wrong with me? Side effects or anything that I don't know of yet?"

Ishmael looked intently at Maggie.

"Side effects and deformities are really more of a complication in males."

The wind had picked up a bit, caressing the scraggly silver moss hanging from the live oaks. Ishmael quit her picking and let the gentle breeze soothe her troubling thoughts.

Maggie shifted to a new area in the thicket that was covered in plump berries. Her bucket was already half full.

"And speaking of males—there's something else I think should be explained," Maggie said. "Now, I'm not trying to justify Joe's aggressive behavior, but you have to understand that on land Joe was like a caged beast."

A thick cloud drifted overhead, obscuring the dappled sunlight that had only moments before been peeking through the trees. Maggie looked at her granddaughter to make sure she was listening.

"You should know, since Hector can't change either, he's tormented by the same mental demons as his father. I've been working with him. Mental training. Yoga. Breathing exercises. Meditation seems to be helping, so we're making progress. But I want you to be aware of Hector's shortcomings in advance because—well—you should be gentle with him. Careful, even. He's extremely volatile."

Ishmael thought of how she'd saved Hector's life the night before.

"I'm pretty sure I can handle myself—"

"I don't think you understand," Maggie said, leaning in. "As charming as he may seem, Hector's mainly interested in one thing." She paused. "He's desperate to know whether you're alpha enough to change him."

Ishmael's mind flashed back to the afternoon before on the dock. She recalled all the things he'd said. He'd challenged her to swim with him. And the night before—his legs were heavy when she'd pulled him out of the water. Was it possible that his lower half had started forming the thick skin of a tail?

Ishmael looked up to find her grandmother's fierce gray eyes staring into her own.

"If you're as powerful as you seem to be, there's a chance you might be the one to change the course of Hector's life. He wants nothing more than to go live in the ocean, take his aquatic form, and be released from this human form, which he perceives as a prison."

"And there's a chance I might be able to transform him?" Ishmael asked. "Isn't that a good thing?"

"Yes, but that's why I'm warning you. As gentle as he can be, I've seen him be equally as aggressive. I want to discourage you from being lured by his ambitions. There's a time and a place for everything, but I think, for now, we shouldn't get his hopes up. The presence of two alphas hasn't worked in the past. And I've made so much progress with Hector. If he gets let down again, I'm not sure I can help him back up."

Ishmael had certainly glimpsed a side of Hector the night before that confirmed Maggie's warnings. She was happy to avoid him—but could he really be that dangerous?

Maggie looked her granddaughter intently in the eye. "To answer your question—yes."

"Wait, you just read my . . ."

Maggie reached over and put her hand on top of Ishmael's.

"Consider yourself warned," Maggie said. "Hector is like a Siren. He's gorgeous, charming, a smooth-talker, yet he has one potentially perilous goal in mind. He can certainly call your ship into the rocks if you're not paying attention."

19

ISHMAEL PULLED HER HAND FROM HER GRANDMOTHER'S and stood, rubbing her temples. She was stunned, scared, and strangely honored, all in the same breath.

She was powerful enough to change Hector?

The deep song of a dove reverberated from a nearby tree; the sound seemed to pound in Ishmael's skull. She felt dizzy with the heat, the lack of sleep, last night's wine, and her racing thoughts.

"Take your shoes off," Maggie said. "In times like this, you need bare feet."

Ishmael felt the cool sponginess of the ground. Leaves adjusted with soft crackles between her toes.

"You'll feel more grounded this way," Maggie said. "Brings the energy back down."

Ishmael nodded. The tactic was working. With her toes in the dirt, she felt herself take a deeper breath, and the world stopped spinning.

"But—if I'm so powerful," she said, "couldn't I change you?"

"You probably can," Maggie said, searching the picnic basket. "But I don't want you to think that's the only reason I'm glad to see you."

Maggie arranged items from the basket on a nearby stump.

"Have a seat," Maggie said. "Let's get some nourishment in you."

Ishmael unwrapped a cinnamon roll and took a bite.

"But aren't you even curious?"

"Curious, yes," Maggie said, handing Ishmael a napkin, "but that's not my main focus. I'm old. And I couldn't leave Lena behind."

"I like Lena," Ishmael said, wiping the icing from her lips. "She's sturdy. Protective. Like the mother ship."

"I agree," Maggie said with a pleasant smile.

Ishmael thought for a moment. "So is Lena a mermaid?"

"No. But I've told her everything. Lena's just one of those remarkable people who is unshakable. She wasn't shocked at all the first time she saw an aquatic human swimming around our dock. She just takes everything in stride."

Maggie sipped lemonade from the thermos.

"I want you to understand that I'm not concerned about going back to my aquatic form now because I've found my place. My place is here. On land. Your mom acts as a matriarch in the water and I act as a matriarch here on land. It all just works out."

"So how did you end up here? In South Carolina?"

"I came to Butler Island because it was as far out to sea as you could possibly get around these parts. I'll admit, it wasn't much of a plan, but it worked out in the long run. I do love it here."

"So did my mother ever live here with you?"

"Sadly, no. And that's probably why we've never been close. We live such different lives; we're bound to have divergent perspectives. It was one of my toughest life decisions, but I knew your mother wanted to grow up in the ocean. I found a nice female who lived off the coast of Bermuda who agreed to adopt Anna."

"So what—you just shipped my mom off to Bermuda?"

"At first, to give Anna a chance to get her bearings in the ocean, I sent her to live with a very small pod of aquatic humans up near Hatteras. Because she was a strong alpha, she changed forms within a few minutes of coexisting with them. And they raised her until she was able to make the crossing over to the larger pod in Bermuda."

"How old was she when she made the crossing?"

"Five."

"What! My mother crossed the Atlantic at age five?"

"Not the entire Atlantic. And she was with an adult, of course. They took their time."

Ishmael couldn't help but smile.

"And she was okay to just leave you?"

"Honestly, I don't think Anna even thought of me once she came to understand the potential of her aquatic form. Your mother *thrives* in the water." Maggie looked off. "I was torn up about it for years. But when I knew I could trust Lena, I poured my heart out to her and I was able to work out my grief and come to understand that I had made the best decision I could."

"That makes me . . . sad."

"Yes." Maggie sighed, and then forced a smile. "But, perhaps you can see why your mother was not distraught in leaving you when you were only six. She figured you were plenty old enough."

"But I don't understand why my parents came to land in the first place. If my mother loved the water so much, why risk—"

"Because of you. She risked it all because of you. Anna wanted her daughter to grow up on land. Get an education, make a life for herself. Aquatic humans are a dying race. She wanted you to be somewhere *you* could thrive."

"You make her sound so heroic."

"Ishmael, I don't think your mother went for a swim that afternoon with the intention of staying in the ocean."

Ishmael swallowed. "What are you saying?"

"She's never outright told me, and our communication is sparse, but I'm betting all my chips on the fact that your mother is not capable of changing back to a human," Maggie said. "I say this because if she could have returned to you, I know she would have. As much as Anna loves the ocean, I've always believed she loves you more."

Ishmael choked on her tears. She bit her lip to stifle the urge to weep.

"I don't think she's ever been able to forgive herself for that," Maggie said. "I think that's why she avoids me. Because she knows that I know the truth and it pains her to see me and face it."

"But I could've forgiven her. We could've visited her."

"You must know that a visit with your *mermaid mother* could've been tricky for your father to arrange." Maggie touched Ishmael's arm. "I know your mother feels terrible for what she did. But I will say I get the sense we are so-called *stuck* where we should be. Whether on land or the water, the process seems to choose where the true work needs to be done."

Ishmael shot up, pulling her hand away.

"I don't know, Maggie." Ishmael paced. "She could've done *something*! Something to show me she wasn't dead! Hell, I could have lived in the ocean with her! If she'd come back for me—just once—I could've swam away with her. She could have at least given me *the choice*."

"There's still time for that," Maggie said.

"What? No. No way. It's too late. I mean—I can't go with her *now*. I'm too old."

Maggie laughed.

"Please spare an old lady like me the excuse that you're *too old*."

"I don't know anything about living in the ocean," Ishmael said. "Or being an aquatic human."

"Hector would argue that you certainly know more than him. He'd do just about anything to know what you know. To feel what you've felt in the water."

Maggie caught her granddaughter's eye.

"Because it does feel exhilarating, doesn't it?" Maggie asked. "Powerful. Liberating."

Ishmael supposed she was going to have to get used to having her thoughts read. Being in her aquatic form was the most liberated feeling she'd had in her entire life.

"I just want you to be proud of your mother," Maggie said. "As I am. Your mother and I aren't always simpatico, but I admire Anna."

A breeze swirled over the dirt road and picked up the end of Maggie's braid. A rumble of thunder resonated in the distance. Maggie stood, looked up at the sky, and put on her hat.

"My goodness. Lena won't like us coming back with only half a bucket of berries. But judging from those clouds, it's time to head on back."

The women gathered their belongings just as a light drizzle started. The wind tossed the trees erratically and kicked up swirls of dust.

"Uh-oh, here we go," Maggie said, holding her hat down in a gust of wind.

The sky opened all at once, and the rain pounded down in sheets.

Ishmael felt the droplets sliding down her cheeks like tears. Within minutes, her entire body was soaked to the bone. The two women leaned forward into the rain and pressed on without speaking, their hair plastered to their faces, their shirts clinging to their skin like tissue paper.

Ishmael welcomed the deluge. She needed to get her thoughts straight. But then she had a terrible thought—the rain, all the wetness—she stopped, still as a statue. She pictured herself writhing on the dirt road with a tail.

Maggie looked back at her granddaughter, water streaming from her straw hat like translucent ribbons.

"You've still got a lot to understand, Ishmael Morgan!" she yelled over the downpour. "Only works in salt water!"

20

THE RAIN LET UP AS THEY APPROACHED THE HOUSE. Ishmael set the buckets down by the back steps.

"I'm going for a swim."

"Might as well. We're soaked already," Maggie said, leaving the soggy picnic basket on the back steps.

Ishmael blinked her eyes as raindrops caught her eyelashes. "You're going with me?"

"Hector was smart enough to drill holes in the bottom of those buckets. Those berries will be washed by the heavens by the time we get back."

"You're sure you want to do this?" Ishmael asked. "Now?"

Maggie passed Ishmael and headed for the dock. "Let's get a move on. Lightning's let up for now. Another storm's on the way."

The rain came down harder and drowned out any chance of discussion as they headed to the creek. Maggie pulled the leather cord from around her neck and dropped her hat on the dock. Ishmael slid out of her shoes and dove in.

She was already soaked, so it wasn't the wetness that was satisfying. It was the confidence she felt in the water, the security. She stripped her pants and threw them in a wet pile on the dock. Maggie secured a ladder she had retrieved from the rafters to make it easier for her to climb in. Ishmael paddled through the water with her arms, relishing the immersion, freshwater droplets tickling her scalp from above.

She felt the change beginning and dove beneath the surface. Underwater, with large sweeping motions of her arms, she pulled herself, tasting the wonderful saltiness on her lips. She closed her eyes and swam deeper into the embrace of the ocean: her mind was empty, all worries gone. As soon as she felt the completion of the shift, she kicked her tail and propelled herself forward, shooting through the water. Her arms trailed by her side, eyes open despite the saltiness, her body pleasantly powerful and capable in this aquatic form. She remembered Maggie, circled back, and surfaced.

"That was quite a long breath hold," Maggie said, leaving the ladder hanging half-secured. Her attention was on Ishmael. "In no time, holding your breath will become even easier. You'll be able to dive deeper. Stay under longer."

The sky had shifted momentarily from gray to gold. The rain came down only as a soft drizzle.

"You coming in?" Ishmael asked.

"Lift your fluke. Let me see it," Maggie said.

Ishmael leaned back in the water, balancing herself with small propulsions of her arms. Her tail surfaced, and she and Maggie both smiled.

"It's breathtaking," Maggie said.

"I would have to agree."

"You know, your mother has been known to accomplish half-hour breath holds."

Ishmael gaped. "Impossible."

Maggie crossed her arms over her chest. "Ever heard of the Ama divers off the coast of Japan?"

She paused to watch Ishmael shake her head.

"You should look them up. Mainly women. Some of them *old* women like me. They dive with no gear, no air tanks. Just their able bodies."

Maggie went back to work on the ladder.

"A long breath hold is about training the mind," Maggie added. "Teaching the mind to stay calm when the diaphragm spasms. You've felt those spasms before. I'm sure you have, and the impulse is to gulp for air. But if you can get past that, the body will recalibrate."

Thunder rumbled in the distance.

"Dad-gum. I never can seem to make this ladder sturdy enough. Not sure what I'm doing wrong. . . . Oh, well. Good enough. No more stalling." She looked toward Ishmael with a grin. "It's now or never."

But an object caught Maggie's eye, and her expression shifted.

"Did you put that crab pot up here?" Maggie asked. "My goodness! Has it been here this *whole time*?"

Ishmael was just now noticing that Hector's big boat was not at the dock. She certainly hadn't noticed a misplaced crab pot.

"Where is it?" Maggie spun around, keeping her eyes focused down on the water. "Have you seen it?"

"Seen what?" Ishmael asked.

"One of them is here. The crab pot on the dock means there's a message for us."

Ishmael's eyes darted across the creek, looking for a ripple or a bubble trail. It was odd to think that another one, like her, had been swimming right under her nose. She was awed by the stealth.

"Maggie, I—"

"There! Look! Two of them!"

Ishmael looked but saw nothing; she only heard Lena's heavy footsteps coming down the dock. Lena seemed in exceptionally good spirits.

"Phew-wee. Leon's gone to pick them clowns up at the boatyard since a storm's brewing. They was *hung-over* in my kitchen this morning! I tell you! They all went out on the boat, though. Thank the Lord. Keep them from lounging around all day eating junk food and messing up my clean house."

Chatty as a cheerleader, just as Maggie had predicted. But Maggie wasn't listening. Maggie seemed to be in a zone, scanning the creek with intense focus.

"Just letting y'all know that we might be eating a little later than usual. Leon's joining us. I invited him. Saw y'all got us some good berries. They'll make us a nice pie."

"Lena, I think Maggie—"

"Looking good, Ishmael."

Lena seemed in no way surprised that Ishmael was in the water with a tail. She walked over to the half-hung ladder and easily adjusted it so that it was secure. Finally, she spied the crab pot, and her eyes darted to Maggie.

"Oh, Lord. Here I am jabbering away!" Lena seemed to shift into another gear. "Shoot, Maggie. I'll head on back up and stall Hector when he gets back."

Lena turned and headed back across the lawn: it was the fastest Ishmael had seen her move.

"Stall who?" Ishmael asked.

There was a loud shrieking noise, and Ishmael felt her skin crawl. She kicked with her tail and shot out of the water, perching herself on the edge of the dock for a better view.

"What the hell was that?"

"They're trying to communicate," Maggie said. "It must be young ones. They don't know the hand gestures."

Ishmael's eyes shot to the water beneath the dock. From the shadows, two faces appeared. Their bodies were fit and sturdy, their shoulders chiseled, their arms defined with ropy muscles even in their youth. A male and a female. The male had the pubescent beginnings of a stubbly beard. The female wore multiple bracelets roughly braided with shells.

Teenagers. Ishmael almost laughed out loud. She remembered being that age. She'd persuaded her dad to buy her a whole slew of neon jelly bracelets. She imagined what a different life these two must lead. There was nothing plastic about them. Their cheeks were radiant with health, their teeth clean, their eyes fierce but bright. Ishmael was enchanted.

The male in the water opened his mouth, and Ishmael cringed. The noise stung, and she slapped her palms over her ears.

"We have to tell them they can't do that," Maggie said when the obnoxious chattering finally stopped. "I don't want Dan showing up asking questions."

Ishmael's mind raced. Dan? Right. *Game warden Dan.*

The shriek came again and both women covered their ears.

"No way Dan didn't hear *that*," Ishmael said.

The screen door slammed. Leon's truck was visible around the back of the house, and Hector was already running across the lawn.

Lena stood in the doorway of the front porch, propping the screen door open with her wide arms.

"I tried! No stopping him!"

Maggie's eyes shot back to the water and she gave an anxious look at the two in the creek. The female responded with a high-pitched chirp.

"You don't have any idea what any of the sounds mean?" Ishmael asked.

"I'm afraid I'm out of the loop with these two."

Ishmael's thick skin was dropping away. She could just reach her wet clothes. She tossed them over her lower half as Hector approached.

"They don't know the gestures," Maggie said to Hector once he reached the dock.

"Yeah, and apparently you two aren't so up to date on your chirps and squeals," Ishmael said.

Hector spun toward Ishmael, his eyes narrow. He nearly growled. Maggie put a hand on Hector's back.

"No, no, no. It's okay," Maggie said in a soothing voice. "We're all calm here. Everything's fine."

Hector was breathing hard, almost gasping.

"What the hell is wrong with him?" Ishmael asked, pulling her T-shirt over her head.

"He'll be okay. Just keep calm." Maggie lowered her voice. "He wants to change and he can't. It's frustration a million times over. Having a male here just exacerbates the situation."

Hector crouched down beside Maggie and set his jaw, staring at her.

"It's true, Hector." Maggie fired back at Hector's wild gaze. "You *must* learn to control this. You'll spend miserable years on land until you can control this. The frustration—it's all in your mind." She tapped her temple with one finger. "*You* are in control."

Hector leapt to standing and paced again on the dock. His breath grew even fiercer. Maggie watched him for a moment, but then she leaned back down apprehensively to the faces in the water. Hector continued to pound his footsteps on the dock. Ishmael sat in panic, watching the bizarre scene.

"I can't believe they sent such young ones to relay information!" Maggie said. "This is preposterous."

Suddenly, another face emerged from the water, sliding gracefully up from the depths. The young ones kicked their tails nervously and slid back in the water.

"A-ha! Here we go," Maggie said.

There was no greeting. Maggie simply knelt down on the dock and held out her arm. The female's thick, long fingernails curled around Maggie's wrist, and she played her fingers in a staccato code across Maggie's forearm. Maggie's expression shifted to concentration as the female typed. Then, as if she had thought of something, the female turned to the smaller male and female and made an abrupt clicking noise. The two younger ones shrunk at the command and dove away. Ishmael watched their bubble trail as they retreated down the creek. The female turned back to Maggie and typed again.

Ishmael watched the typing curiously. "Maggie, how can you possibly get any information from that?"

"It's basically Morse code. It was developed when aquatics first starting coming to land. It's rudimentary, but it gets the point across."

Maggie's eyes shot to Hector.

"It's your father," she said. "It's Joe."

Hector stopped pacing. The female typed again.

"Joe is—" Maggie turned to look back at Hector. "Hector—he's dead."

The female glanced beyond Maggie's shoulder in Hector's direction. Hector stood rigid, his only movement the heaving of his chest. The female typed again. Maggie gulped and covered her hand with her mouth.

"What is it?" Hector asked.

Maggie pulled her arm away. The female dropped back down into the water and hovered, only her shoulders above the surface.

"I'm afraid there's more," Maggie said, pushing on her knees to stand. "Hector, they know because they found him in the water. And when they found him—well, Hector—his body was half changed."

Hector's eyes blazed with confusion.

"The greater problem is that the aquatic ones left him," Maggie said. "And others found him."

"Others?" Hector shouted, looking beyond Maggie to the female for an answer. "Who? Who found him?"

The female merely hovered quietly in the water, unalarmed by Hector's tantrum.

"Humans," Maggie reported. "Humans found him. He won't change back to full human after he's dead—even if he dries out. The changes will stay."

"How far along was he?" Hector asked.

Maggie looked at Hector sympathetically. "One foot was a fin, the other had webbing." She sighed and added, "Tougher skin in patches. No fluke. No binding of the tail."

"Where was he?"

"Atlantic side of Panama. Fishing boat found him floating offshore."

Ishmael was silent. She was too overwhelmed to speak.

"How?" Hector asked. He swallowed, obviously trying to quell his own emotion at the news. He shook his head. "Joe couldn't—not possible," he said, his eyes damp with angry tears. Storming across the dock, he punched a piling but then spun around. Eyes narrowed, he asked, "What does this mean for me?"

Maggie shook her head. "I honestly don't know."

Lightning flashed in the distance. A black storm cloud was forming on the horizon. Maggie turned to the female for an official answer. It was obvious from the female's expression that she had more to say. Hector rushed over, bent down and offered the female his arm. The female rose again in the water, exposing the place just beneath her navel where the thick skin began. Ishmael was enthralled, maybe even a little impressed to see Hector so comfortable with this glorious creature. It was obvious that he comprehended all that was being typed so furiously on his forearm.

The female dropped back into the water with barely a ripple, but Hector remained crouched on all fours and dropped his head in defeat. His body shuddered, and Ishmael saw he was crying. She approached him, but Maggie grasped her arm and stopped her.

"What did she tell him?" Ishmael asked.

"I'm sure only more of what she told me," Maggie said. She turned to look at her granddaughter. "Joe Cruz was found with an alpha female. A young one. More powerful. That's how Joe was able to change." She shook her head, her face ashen, her eyes fragile with disdain. "The female had been strangled. They think Joe might have killed her."

"Did the humans find the female?"

"No. Luckily, our kind found her first. They only left Joe floating out of complete contempt. But it was a careless mistake. His body should've never been found like that."

"So what happens now?"

"We wait. No telling how the humans will respond. There's nothing we can do."

Hector stood, keeping his back to Maggie and Ishmael.

Maggie looked his way briefly but then turned her attention back to the creek, nodding to the female in the water. "She should get going, Hector."

She walked across the dock and dropped the crab pot back in the water. The female turned with a chirp, dove, and was gone. Maggie returned to Hector and set a hand on his shoulder. He shook it off and stormed up the ramp: the door to the dock house slammed moments later.

"I should go talk to him," Ishmael said.

"He's better off alone for a bit," Maggie said.

Allen and Diane were crossing the lawn.

"But he's upset."

"Trust me. He needs to cool off before anyone goes in there," Maggie said.

Ishmael looked uneasily toward the dock house. Diane rushed down the ramp, Allen in tow.

"I brought towels!" Diane proclaimed. A waft of sunscreen and perfume came down the dock with her. "What'd we miss? Something about a crab pot?"

Ishmael stood, two legs restored, and wrapped a towel around her waist.

Allen walked straight to Ishmael.

"Ish—you okay?" he asked.

"Well, excitement's over. Nothing to see here," Maggie said, putting a hand on Diane's back, guiding her back toward the ramp.

"We should be getting back up to the house. Another storm's on the way."

"Well, hold on—what about—?" Diane stumbled, not wanting to leave the dock.

"I think we should give these two a moment alone," Maggie said. Ishmael called after them. "Maggie, I'm sorry we didn't get to—"

"That's the least of my concerns," Maggie said, gently corralling Diane off the dock.

"We'll be up there in a few," Allen said. He watched Diane and Maggie leave the dock. Turning back to Ishmael, his eyes were desperate. His hand gripped her arm a little too tightly.

"Hector told me about your mother, Ish. How they've sent word out for her." He exhaled, examining her expression. His shoulders relaxed. "I thought that was her in the water."

"My mother?" Ishmael smiled, butterflies loose in her ribcage at the possibility. She bit her lip to contain the sudden rush of hope. "No, it wasn't her."

"I just wanted a chance to talk to you first. Because if it was your mother—I wouldn't want to—"

He looked her in the eye. He seemed nervous.

"I just wanted to mention the people on *land* who love you."

She looked back at him.

"Like me," he said.

She bit her lip and took a deep breath.

"Look—Allen, you've got to know that I have no idea what comes next these days. But whatever I choose to do, you can't expect—"

He moved closer and gripped her upper arms.

"I know that," he said. "I know. What I'm trying to say is—"

He dropped his arms and stood straighter.

"I love you," he said.

His voice remained strong.

"And I know you don't love me back."

Her heart plunged at the truth. She was grateful he had spoken the words.

He stepped back and faked a smile.

"And it's okay. I'll live," he said. "But I want you to know that I will always love you. Always."

He turned and walked away. He crossed the lawn back to the house. Ishmael was alone on the dock.

She sighed, rubbed her stubble of hair. A breeze ripped through the trees, and the scent of honeysuckle filled her nose. She breathed deeply, grateful for the sweetness in the air to lighten the heaviness she felt in her heart. She readjusted her wet shirt and knelt to gather the rest of her clothes from the dock. She stood, startled at the sight of Hector standing at the top of the ramp.

"You hungry?" he asked.

Damn straight, she was. She'd only eaten a cinnamon roll and a handful of blackberries all day.

Hector leaned into his forearms on the railing, and the creases of his muscles revealed themselves like ripples on a perfectly iced cake. His eyes were docile, relaxed. This was Hector. Her childhood friend, suddenly and mysteriously dangerous.

He put a hand on her back when she reached the upper dock.

"Figured we could both use the company," he said.

After all she'd been through, after all she now knew, the touch of his hand on her back was comforting. Like she was back in the water, her mind clear, her worries temporarily evaporated.

Perhaps she was a fool, but she followed him off the dock.

21

THIS WAS A DIFFERENT ROOM FROM THE NIGHT BEFORE. Posters, maps, and newspaper clippings still blanketed the walls, but books were shelved, the bed was made, the table was set, the furniture straightened. After the cool rain, the windows were open. Curtains fluttered against screens in the fresh breeze.

"Here, take these." Hector held out some dry clothes.

She couldn't read his expression, but he didn't seem apologetic or guilty. *Did he not remember last night at all? Not even a dim recollection?*

"Feel free to use the bathroom to change," he said. "I'll hang your wet clothes on the line."

In the bathroom, she slid his dry cotton T-shirt over her head. The front advertised a shrimping business and had a picture of a large trawler with sweeping nets on the back. The pants were drawstring sweatpants, baggy and certainly not flattering. Looking in the mirror, she chuckled to imagine Diane's opinion of this outfit. A familiar, pleasant scent filled her nostrils. His laundry detergent.

Clean, with a hint of spice.

She slipped back into the main room. "Smells great," she said. His back was turned as he worked at the stove.

"Look, ah, I'm really sorry about your—about Joe," she added.

He exhaled. "Me too. I kind of thought—" He shook his head. "Actually, no. Doesn't surprise me. But it makes me nauseous. Nauseous and terrified." He looked at her. "Can you do us a favor, though? Can we talk about anything else besides . . . that? I haven't seen or heard from the guy in almost fifteen years. He's screwed up my life enough at this point—I have no desire to let him mess up this evening."

"Of course. Yeah, sure."

He forced a smile.

"Hey, I'm not drinking, but would you like a glass of wine?" He started to pour the glass of red wine without even waiting for her response. "We're having fish, but this is an amazing pinot. I'll get you a glass of white with dinner."

He lifted the glass of wine to her and smiled briefly before returning to his cooking. Ishmael sipped the wine, peering more closely around the room. For the first time, she noticed the painting hanging over his bed. It was hers.

"Whoa, how did you—I had that hanging in the Santorini Gallery."

Your dad gave me that painting." Hector didn't even look up, busy in the kitchen.

She squinted. "My dad's been gone over ten years."

He paused in his prep work, choosing his words.

"Ish, your dad wasn't exactly thrilled when you started sleeping with his best friend." He looked over to check her reaction. "But that's not the only reason he took off."

She felt herself blush, so she turned back to the painting.

"So you know about me and Allen."

"You and El Padre dated for what, four years?"

He tasted from one of the pots on the front burner and added more spices. He seemed totally relaxed. After the talk about Richard and Allen, she felt the opposite, so she took heavy sips of the wine as she approached her painting.

"I love your work," Hector said. He paused and gazed at the painting with her. "This piece just gives me such a sense of looking up at the sun or the moon from underwater. You know what I mean?"

She'd never thought of that, but now it was so clear. Of course.

This painting in particular, mostly eggplant purples and peacock blues, gave rise to a single luminescent, crimson sphere. The gentle splattering of primrose yellow could have been the intricate foam of the ocean. Or dappled light reflecting off waves of pigment. The thick paint was dimpled at a specific angle, as if a strong wind had blown across the surface of the wet colorant and it had dried, held in place on the canvas. Proof of something so intangible as a breeze.

"I painted this one in the trailer park," she said.

He smiled, apparently enjoying the chance to see the artist and painting reunited in his apartment.

"This was one of the last I painted there, before I got a real studio," she continued, energized by the flood of memories. "There's just something about the pieces I painted in the trailer park. They're so raw." She laughed softly. "I hadn't been cooked by the art world yet." She glanced back at him. "Make any sense to you?"

He nodded. "Absolutely."

She sipped her wine, looking beyond her painting and into the past. "I wasn't holding back in any way whatsoever. No commitments. No rules. Just unedited passion. An absolute *need* to create."

He was staring at her.

"What? I'm talking too much, aren't I? I'm getting too artsy for you."

"No! No—hell no," he said. "It's the most I've heard you talk since you got here. I should've known this was the way to get you to open up. Talk about art."

She felt her face flush. No one had ever taken the time to listen to her talk about her paintings. She moved to the couch and sipped the wine.

"I still can't believe you have one of my paintings," she said.

"Richard kept tabs on his famous artist daughter. When he heard your stuff went into a legit gallery, he called the place and they emailed him a few images of your stuff. But I think your dad looked only at dimensions—he bought the biggest one."

She sat forward. "My dad knows about the internet? Wait— no, correction—my dad knows what a computer is?"

"Ish, your dad's a really smart guy. He chooses to live the simple life. He's not forced to."

"That was not a cheap painting."

"He has some funds stashed away."

She sat back. "How can I not know all this stuff?"

"You were a little lost in your own world. And rightly so. You'd lost your mom. And you had an antisocial dad. Then you spent all that time at the coffee shop. You were, what, sixteen when you started working there? You were so immersed in that job. It's no wonder El Padre fell in love with you." He checked something in the oven and then added. "Your dad used to come to my soccer games while you were at work."

"My dad."

"He also helped coach football one season."

"Football?"

"Ish, your dad was six foot five inches and pushing two-fifty. He wasn't an expert on the game by any means, but he knew how to keep us fit. He trained us. We won all-state that year. He had us in incredible shape."

She gaped and then sat back.

"I feel like such a . . ." Her voice trailed off. She wasn't ready to admit her fault in the distance between her and her dad.

Hector donned a mitt and pulled a tray from the oven.

"The painting came in this gigantic crate," he said. "Richard had to send it to Leon's produce stand since all Maggie's got is a PO box. Arrived two days before my thirtieth birthday."

"Typical that Richard sent birthday presents to you and not his own daughter."

He turned from the pot he was stirring.

"I thought that might make you mad. It shouldn't."

He turned back to the stove.

"It was just that one time. And I honestly think your dad wanted to support you. But what was he going to do with a painting?" He pointed at the wide canvas over his bed. "Hang *that* in his camper?"

"Unbelievable. I didn't know my dad had it in him."

"You've got the wrong idea about your dad," he said. "When we were growing up, all the *groms* used to worship him. And I was right there with them. Your dad was like our hero. He was quiet, sure, but he surfed the biggest, gnarliest swells that came through Encinitas, even when his beard was nothing but gray." He looked up in honest reverence. "I've never seen anyone read the ocean like he did."

He turned back to his cooking, a dishrag slung over one shoulder. The towel was a prop that seemed familiar to him, evidence that he was comfortable in the kitchen. He dragged milky-white strips of fish through a batter and breadcrumbs and then placed the fillets into a pan of oil. The pan hissed each time he added another strip.

"So, what's next for Ish Morgan?"

He asked his question in a friendly manner, but she was caught off guard. She set her glass down, welcoming any movement that prolonged her answer.

"Not too sure," she said, ignoring his gaze. She wondered if he had overheard her conversation with Allen. A nervous laugh came out before she could stop herself. "Got any suggestions, be my guest."

He waited a moment and then said, "You're tough. And you've got the whole aquatic thing down. I guess I just assumed—"

"You saw me last night, didn't you? In the water."

"I was pretty hammered, but bits and pieces have come back to me. Luckily." He turned to her. "By the way, speaking of last night, did I—?"

He caught her gaze and saw the answer in her eyes.

"And so you saved me?" he asked.

She tried to play it cool, but she found herself fidgeting.

"I thought I'd dreamt all that," he said. "I thought I was having some sort of fantasy about you—us—I mean—"

"Yeah. Yes. You did—I did. I'm pretty sure I—well, I—I guess I saved your life. I mean, you fell off the dock and—" *Ishmael! Pull yourself together.*

"Did you resuscitate me?" he asked. "I feel like such a dumbass. Look, I'm really sorry. Here—maybe this will get me some sympathy." He parted his hair to show her a large knot on his head. Then, he lifted his shirt. "I'm pretty sure that I also broke the bottle of liquor I was drinking. I'm assuming that's why I have these cuts and scrapes all over me. Told Lena they were cuts from oyster shells, which most likely didn't fool her for a second, but she played along."

She looked at his body and lost all concentration.

"Ah—yep, you broke it. The bottle. I, ah—I swept up the glass."

She had to pull herself together.

He stepped toward her, away from his cooking. "Did you get cut?"

"Only a little. It's fine."

He stepped even closer.

"It's fine," she said. "Really. Just a scratch."

"I'm so sorry, Ish. You saved my life. I'm an asshole. I don't know what to say. I promise I'll be on my best behavior tonight." He cocked a grin. "You're seriously brave, you know that?"

"Brave?" She laughed, picking up her wine. "Think you got the wrong girl."

"Pretty darn brave of you to swim back from Baja and ditch your fiancé," he said, turning back to his fish on the stove. "Brave of you to travel across the country to find your long-lost grandmother."

"Yeah, well, I wasn't brave enough to call my fiancé and tell him the truth." She lowered the glass from her lips. "Hold up—how do you know about Nicholas?"

"Maggie." He turned back to his cooking and spoke over his shoulder. "I'm sure you know by now—Maggie knows all."

"Well, I'm pretty sure I should've at least told him I'm not dead."

"I totally disagree," he said, covering a plate with a folded paper towel. "Involving Nicholas would've only added more headaches to your plate. You're doing the best you can."

He pulled a few strips of fish out of the oil and put them on the plate with the paper towel covering.

"Not to mention, could you have trusted Nicholas with the truth? He never would have believed you—and if you'd shown him, he probably would have freaked out and left." He looked at her. "No, Ish. You did the right thing. It took guts to do what you did. Sometimes the right thing just feels like the wrong thing."

He turned back to the final pieces of fish still in the pan, adjusting the temperature on the stove.

"Let's not forget that it was pretty damn brave of you to buzz your head. And you're definitely pulling that look off."

She gulped the remainder of her wine.

Was he flirting? Yes, definitely, he was flirting.

"So you know everything?" she asked.

"Pretty much."

"Then you must know that I'm some sort of alpha female or something?"

He glanced over his shoulder at her from the kitchen.

"Yes, I do. And I also know you've survived enough to make most women crumble." He smiled at her and added, "Basically—I know I'm impressed."

She felt a tingle at the compliment. She lifted her empty wine glass to her lips to hide her smile. She was acting like she was in the eighth grade again: Maggie had warned her about this.

Whatever. That was the least of her concerns right now. She was busy appreciating that for the first time in weeks, her mind was clear, or at least not racing. Okay, okay—maybe it was the alcohol, but she felt comfortable. Safe. He knew everything. What a relief. To talk to someone who knew the whole story and who accepted her.

"Okay, so you've impressed me," he declared, turning with plated food in both hands, "Now, hopefully, I can impress you."

She walked over to the table. A fresh glass of chilled white wine was already poured. He took her empty red wine glass and pulled the chair out for her.

The food was phenomenal. He had prepared a meal highlighting the very best of local fare—a fresh tomato pie, cheese grits, delicately fried flounder, and a crisp salad with cucumbers and radishes from the garden. She went back for a second helping. They talked about his job at the boatyard and her paintings and reminisced about the trailer park.

There was an ebullient mood at the dinner table, and the conversation was lighthearted, flirty, and fun. She was clearly having a good time, and he seemed enthralled with her every word. She welcomed the attention after so many days stranded alone in her thoughts. They stood to clear the table, and she insisted on helping with the dishes. In the small kitchen, their elbows grazed one another; their shoulders touched. The simple contact of their skin made her heart flutter.

He glanced toward her. She tried to pull her eyes away, but he held her gaze. Outside, the rain poured in sheets, shielding them from visitors, pattering on the metal roof, blocking out all noises of the reality beyond the screens. Hector turned the water off and took her face in his hands. His fingers smelled pleasantly of soap. Citrus, with just a hint of lavender. His stare was cool and deep as a well.

She was suddenly overcome by lust, by how much she wanted him. The plate slid from her hands and she wrapped her arms around his neck. He pulled her in closer. Their bodies pressed together. His lips grazed her mouth.

She stretched her hands across his back, spreading her fingers, pressing him even tighter. Their heads tilted, merging their faces, locking their lips. A long kiss. A kiss that made her feel as if she were riding a wave all the way to the shore, lifted and suspended and swept away all at the same time. She felt unsteady, as if the surface beneath her were surging, billowing.

He reached a hand and searched for the cord to the blinds. One yank and the blinds tilted closed. She lifted his shirt as he tugged the drawstring on her pants. His brawny hands immediately glided across the back of her thighs, and she felt delicate and powerful at the same time. They continued kissing, his strong hands holding her cheeks, cradling her face like a treasure he would never let go.

They stumbled instinctively across the room, him leading the way to his bed with a tender tug, his lips still moving all over her face and neck. The eagerness between them hummed, vibrated. They fell onto the bed and became a coil of arms and legs, bodies spliced, desires intertwined.

He slid his hand up her shirt. His nuzzling was gentle, smooth, but as they continued to kiss, the tenderness dropped away, the caresses became all at once combustible, his mild strokes slipped into a fiery aggression. Abruptly, he groped and pinched and pushed her with exacerbated fervor.

She pressed her hands on his bare chest, turning her head to peel his lips from hers, shoving him away.

"Easy there, tiger," she said.

He was disoriented. "What? What's wrong?"

She looked at him with a muddled expression. "You were being so—you were being sweet and then all of a sudden you started—you were kind of hurting me."

His face collapsed, and she gently put her hands back on his chest.

"It's okay," she said. "Let's just slow it down a bit. We'll get there."

He moved back toward her slowly. He kissed her again, this time more softly. She relaxed back into the rhythm of their bodies, overcome by the way he moved so perfectly with her. The pleasure was excruciating.

Until the movements changed again. He pushed up onto his hands and took heaving breaths. She opened her eyes at the panting and saw that his eyes were remote, glassed-over. The anger was back. He was hurting her.

"Hector!"

He didn't respond.

"Hector, stop!"

He didn't.

She screamed, only fueling his rage. She yelled, screeched, and thrust him back, punching him in the chest. He rolled off and lay panting beside her.

"What the hell just happened!" she yelled.

He turned his eyes away and said nothing.

"Holy shit! You seem so—it's like you *hate* me."

He turned back to look at her, black irises reminding her of a moonless sky.

"I do," he said.

"*You hate me*?"

"No. Not really. Not all of me."

"What the hell for?" She sat up, resting on an elbow, trying to glean clues from his face. "What could possibly make you *that mad*?"

He looked over at her, his chest still heaving.

"You know I can't change," he said.

"That's *it*? That's what made you get so rough with me?" She was mad now. "The land isn't such a terrible place, Hector. It was only weeks ago that I found out I had this—*aquatic option*—in my life." She threw her hands up. "And I'm not even sure I want it."

"Grass is always greener," he said. He started to get out of bed, but she stopped him.

"Wait! What the—the grass is always greener! *Are you freaking kidding me*? You don't have to live down this dirt road with these two old ladies. You can go anywhere. Do anything. I don't get it. Why do you stay here?"

"There's more to it."

"Like *what*?"

He said nothing.

"Tell me. I seriously want to know."

He turned and looked at her with a tentative expression. "It's different for the males."

"In what way? Elaborate, please."

He searched for the words, rubbing his head with his hands. "If a male can't change, it causes more—" He looked up. "I don't know—it can be aggravating. Torturous."

She sat back against the headboard. Déjà vu. Maggie had talked to her about this.

"Look." His eyes pleaded with her. "I—I don't know what to say. I keep messing this up. But, god, I like you. And I'm so *so* sorry."

He pushed his long hair back from his face.

"I hate to use the excuse that I can't help it," he said, "but—*shit*—that sounds like such a *stupid* excuse."

"Then please don't give me a stupid excuse," she pleaded. "Find a better one. Make me understand."

He released a colossal exhale.

"Ish, I really have a problem." He looked down. "I'm only mad because I'm jealous as hell of you. And that's childish. Completely childish." He looked back at her. "And all I can say is that I'm doing my best. I'm working on it. The anger. With all I've got. I won't let it overcome me like it overcame my dad. I refuse to let that happen."

He stood from the bed and retrieved the shorts he had been wearing before.

"I'm just so sorry I made you the victim of this torture. I really am, Ish. I am *so sorry*."

He came back and sat on the bed beside her.

"So what do we do here?" she asked. "With this? With us?"

"Maggie's helping me," he said. "She's mastered it—this aggression thing—so I figured I can too."

"I can't imagine Maggie aggressive."

"Lena saved her. And now hopefully Maggie can save me. She's my rock. My hope."

He looked at her, uncomfortable with the admission.

"It'll be harder for me because I'm a guy, but she's coaching me. And that's why I stick around here. That's why I live down a dirt road with two old ladies."

He rose from the bed and leaned against the sink, giving her space. His shirt was off and his arms flexed as he pressed his hands into the counter. He was backlit by the dim glow of a dock light coming through the tilted blinds. The gloaming softened her perspective. She couldn't help but admire the muscular waves of his stomach. She knew it was crazy, but she was already forgiving his unforgivable behavior.

"I do realize this is not a turn on," he said.

"Hector, I'm—" She hesitated before she admitted this to him. "I'm really attracted to you. But what just happened—"

"Ish, you don't have to explain. I can't apologize enough." He held his hands up. "No more fooling around. I promise. Not until I can get myself under control." He shrugged. His broad shoulders glistened with a silky sweat.

"You just—you turn me on." He looked at her. "In a good way," he said quickly. "But the way you kiss me—it brings too much to the surface."

She couldn't believe she was falling for this. She couldn't believe she was letting him back in.

"I could apologize all night," he said.

"Don't."

"I'll do it if that's what it takes," he said.

"Look, Hector—I'm not sure what to think, but—"

He gazed back at her, intently waiting.

She shook her head. "I certainly don't plan to sit here all night with you begging for forgiveness."

"More than you know, I'm grateful." He paused and then added, "I really like you, Ishmael."

He retrieved her clothes from around the room and delivered them to her. While she dressed, he peeked out the blinds.

"Rain's let up," he said.

He turned to her.

"Would you care to join me on the dock?" He smiled. "Away from the bed. Go cool off in the night air."

Once they were down on the dock, he used the dishrag he'd slung over his shoulder to dry two seats for them on the benches. The sun had just set, and the sky was darkening from lavender to indigo. Stars began to appear. In the wake of the storm, the slightest of breezes kept the mosquitoes at bay.

She gazed at the scenery, enjoying the cool air on her face. He slid his hand into hers. She'd wondered how these hands felt. The answer was, perfect. His hand felt perfect in hers. Sturdy. Manly. Strong.

Hector turned to her, looked her in the eyes.

"How about we take a swim?" he asked.

22

SHE TILTED HER HEAD BACK, pretending to look at the stars. Maggie's warnings rushed into her bloodstream as if his question were a needle, injecting her.

"Come on," he said. "You know I'm curious."

The relaxed hold she had on the situation was gone. She sat up straighter.

"We just ate," she said. "Isn't there a rule or something?"

He was already standing. He stripped his clothes, offering one glimpse of his tanned back, the contrast highlighting his pale rear, and dove into the water. The sound of his splash was tempting.

"Come on!" he said, swatting water in her direction. "I know you're not afraid."

She stood, tasting the salty droplets. Of course she would get in the water. She adored being in the water these days. It was where she felt most comfortable, where her problems seemed to melt away. She stripped her clothes and dove in the creek to join him. When she surfaced, he was right beside her, treading water with his hands, looking her in the eye.

"Let's see what you got," he said, smiling.

They swam together through the dark water, stirring up neon twinkles of phosphorescence. They both paddled with their arms, legs dragging, heads above the water. She waited for the feeling, the wrapping sensation, but nothing happened.

"Give it some time," he said, noticing her agitation.

"It's never taken this long," she said. "What's wrong? What am I doing differently?"

"It's probably just the wine. Keep swimming," he said. The soft lapping of the water seemed to have calmed him.

She huffed but kept moving. They continued until the dock light was a small spot behind them.

She stopped. "This isn't right. Something's wrong. What the— it's not happening!"

"Don't get worked up." He treaded water, his voice attempting a soothing tone. "I need you to stay calm. I can't stay calm unless you stay calm."

"How can I stay calm! This is—"

"I'm sure there's a logical—" His voice stopped. "Ish, I think I'm feeling it." He looked at her, his eyes exuberant.

She held her breath and felt for the sensation in her own body. Still nothing. How could he be feeling it and not her? Is this what Maggie had said could happen? She couldn't change anymore but she could still be a catalyst for others. If this was the case, Ishmael anticipated heartbreak.

"What's going on?" Her voice was strained. "What'd you do? How can you be changing and not me?"

He treaded water with his arms, lifting his legs to watch the progress.

"What—you're accusing me? What do you think I did—stir some magic potion in your food?"

His eyes remained mesmerized by his lower half, and she followed his gaze. It was dark, but his legs seemed to be fully bound now, his toes just stretching into a fluke.

She was overwrought: in the moment, she would give anything to take that form again.

"Took it all for granted, didn't you?" he asked.

She felt sick.

"I just don't understand . . ."

Her voice trickled away. The world seemed to tighten around her; her heart thrashed in the confines of her chest. Was this really how it ended? Stuck on land, just like her grandmother? She wanted to scream.

Wait. That was it. She looked at Hector with a broad smile.

"It's happening."

She dove and kicked beneath the surface, shot through the water and breached, soaring above the creek in the moonlight as she bent her body into a backbend and dove backwards into the creek. She spun and twirled, playful in the water that enveloped her and welcomed her home.

When she surfaced, Hector was nowhere in sight. She whirled in all directions, looking for him, and finally caught sight of his head above the water, making his way back to the dock. She swam easily to catch up with him. When she surfaced beside him, he kept his eyes forward, his jaw set.

"What's wrong? Where are you going?" she asked. "I thought this is what you wanted."

He sunk underwater, ignoring her. Even beneath the dark water, she could see his struggle to swim. He wasn't using his tail, only his arms. He reached the dock and pulled himself onto the stern of the small boat. The skin of his lower half had transformed to a deep slate color. Gunmetal gray. Perfect with his skin, his dark hair. He was a masterpiece. She'd never been so magnetized.

"Incomplete," he said, maneuvering himself into a seat on the boat. "And powerless."

"But it happened." She swam closer. "And you're not—"

His feet were still mostly human. Stretched only a bit. His ten toes were flattened but remained unconnected nubs. His heels still intact.

"No, I'm not. Not fully." He shook his head, shaking off the anger. "Hell, it's a start. 'Maybe' is better than a definite 'no.'"

"Hector, I'm so sorry." She tried to look him in the eye. "Honestly, I am. I mean—back there, when I couldn't change—I can imagine how frustrating this must be for you."

He breathed heavily and forced a smile.

"I'm happy for you. At least I'm trying to be. You're incredible in this form. You're perfection like this," he said, gesturing off down the creek. "What you just did out there—the tricks, the dives—this is where you should be, Ish."

He swung his legs over the back of the boat, already starting to separate. Prying his legs apart, he sloughed off the excess thick skin. Pieces fell through the dock boards and into the creek. Since his fluke hadn't fully formed, his feet returned quickly. He stood to retrieve his clothes from the pile and started to dress.

"You're just giving up?" she asked.

"Yup."

"Stay in the water. Give it more time—"

"I'm done for the night." He began to ascend the ramp toward the dock house. "Keep swimming, though," he called back. "Really. It's fine."

"It's not *fine*, Hector. You're pissed."

He said nothing.

"Come *on*. Come back. Talk to me."

She heard him getting a towel from the outside cabinet, saw him tussling his hair to dry it. Then the door closed behind him. Her mind flashed again for one brief moment to his anger before. She had truly been unnerved, but she had to follow him.

She lifted herself onto the edge of the dock and hoisted her tail out of the water.

It had just started drizzling again when she knocked on the door to the dock house. Hearing no response, she turned the doorknob. Hector was inside finishing the dishes. With the water running, maybe he hadn't heard the knock: either that or he'd chosen to ignore her.

She came into the room and leaned against the counter, tipping her head so she could see his face. His eyes were focused on the sink.

"Hey. Can we talk?" she asked.

He ran the water for a moment longer and then shut off the faucet, his eyes avoiding hers, shifting from the dishes to the window above the sink.

"Can I at least help you finish cleaning up?" she asked, gathering the final dishes from the table and placing them beside the sink.

He went back to his cleaning, but eventually he looked up, turning the faucet off again.

"Stay here with me tonight," he said.

She couldn't look up at him.

"I promise—we'll just sleep," he said. He tilted his head to catch her eyes and added, "I'll turn on the AC." He dried his hands on the dishrag and then handed the towel to her. "I just want you in bed with me. I want you all to myself for a night."

She suppressed a smile and nodded.

"Comes with breakfast in the morning," he said, to persuade her. "You've got to let me cook you breakfast. My specialty."

He tenderly touched her face and kissed her on the cheek.

23

HER EYES FLUTTERED OPEN AFTER A DREAM OF FALLING: a nightmare. She was tumbling, plummeting endlessly, helpless. She awoke startled, her breath heavy. It took her a moment to get her bearings, to remember the night before.

Hector barely stirred as she slid out of bed. She walked across the room to the sink and filled a cup with water. As she took a sip, she pushed down one slat of the blinds and peeked through. The sky outside was still dark.

Allen had been in her dream. She hated that at a time like this she was thinking of Allen, but she was. She leaned against the counter, sipping the water. Maybe this wasn't the best time for Allen to find out that she had spent the night with Hector. If she woke up in the guest bedroom, back in the white house, Allen might be in a better mood. Then she could talk to him, encourage him to take Diane and drive back to California—without her.

She'd decided to stay at her grandmother's for at least another week. Hell, if not longer. This was the safest place for her. She was protected here. And she needed a little more time to gather her thoughts before she made her next move. Plus, she couldn't deny it. She wanted more time with Hector.

She dressed in the darkness and snuck out the door, creeping across the dew-dampened lawn just as the sky was beginning to fade from black to violet. The tide was low, emanating the sulphurous scent of pluff mud and marsh grass. Oyster beds lay exposed, ivory mud-coated outcrops barely illuminated in the first utterances of dawn. A few birds were just starting to murmur and shuffle in the leaves of the oak trees as she eased the screen door open. She slinked down the hall of the white house and slid into bed with hardly a sound. Satisfied with her stealth, she was taking a deep breath when Diane spoke.

"There was a curious message on my phone yesterday."

Ishmael's eyes shot open.

"You can imagine my surprise," Diane added.

Ishmael sat up in bed. She'd forgotten all about her drunk dialing. Diane was turned away in the adjacent twin bed. Luckily, she couldn't see Ishmael's expression.

"And I'm not against you calling him, sugar-pie. If that's what you feel is the right thing to do. Just not after drinking a bottle of wine. That could get you in a whole heap of trouble. You know what they say about loose lips? They sink ships, honey."

Ishmael waited until she gained the courage to ask.

"So—he called back?"

Diane shifted to face Ishmael.

"That Nicholas has a smooth voice. He left a very nice message."

"Well? What'd he say?"

Diane kept her eyes closed as she talked.

"He said he didn't recognize the number, but he recognized

my voice on the greeting, and he was glad I called and hoped to talk to me soon."

"Are you going to call him back?"

"Of course. I have to." Diane opened one eye. "I called him *first*."

"But you didn't really. It could be an honest mistake. A mis-dialed number or something."

"Sugar—I don't think that covers it." Diane yawned. "Nicholas Santorini's number wasn't in my phone."

"Shit."

"I agree wholeheartedly. Now let's get back to sleep."

"Does this give me away?"

"I don't think he'll suspect anything with you," Diane said. "What he'll suspect is that something is up with *me*. He thinks I called him at ten o'clock on a Saturday night. That looks a little— shall we say—*unprofessional* at my ripened age."

Saturday night? It wasn't just any Saturday night. It was supposed to be their wedding night. Thankfully, Diane didn't seem to remember that fact.

"I'm sorry, Diane. It was really stupid of me."

"I've weathered worse storms. I'll take care of it. I'll think of something polite and charming to say like I always do."

There was a long pause. Ishmael couldn't help but ask.

"On the voicemail—did he sound—okay?"

Diane sighed. "He sounded like a guy who had lost the love of his life."

Ishmael felt the guilt trapped in her chest. "*Damnit.* I didn't mean to—"

Diane turned over. "I know you didn't, sugar. Breaking hearts is awful work. But if it ain't true love, it's got to be done. And you might go to Hades for pawning that ring, but if it's any consolation,

I think you're doing the right thing. I can't believe I'm saying that after hearing that poor man's voice on that message, but you've got a lot more to work out before you go committing to a marriage."

Ishmael rested her heavy head on the pillow, deep in thought.

"By the way, you're home awful early. What's the scoop?" Diane asked.

Ishmael winced. "Not one to kiss and tell."

"Who said anything about kissing?" Diane smirked, nestling deeper into the covers and closing her eyes again. "Well, I'm liking the sound of this. Can't wait." Diane repositioned herself on the pillow. "Save me all the raunchy details for the morning."

"It is morning," Ishmael said. "And no details."

Diane rolled back over, turning away again.

"Sugar," she said, yawning, "Morning is when the sun comes up."

Diane dozed back into her slumber and was soon snoring. Ishmael closed her eyes and eventually floated into a restless sleep.

◆ ◆ ◆

Ishmael groggily blinked her eyes open to see Diane on the edge of the bed clasping a coffee mug.

"Morning, sunshine," Diane said as she sipped. "So, how was he?"

Ishmael clamped her eyes shut.

"It's complicated."

"You're telling me that you spent the night in that gorgeous man's apartment—after he cooked you dinner—and you didn't sleep with him?"

Ishmael rolled over.

"We slept in the same bed, if that's what you're asking."

"That is most definitely *not* what I'm asking." Diane blew into her mug. "So is he perfect? Looks perfect to me."

Ishmael remained rolled on her side, her back to Diane. Her mind drifted to the night before, when Hector had become so aggressive.

"Perfect's maybe not the best word to use."

"He's got to be damn *close* to perfect."

"You said he'd have baggage, and he does."

"I'm pretty sure that man could have a whole damn turnstile of baggage and I would've done exactly what you did." She sipped her coffee. "Just that drinking problem we might have to work on."

"He didn't drink last night."

Diane set her coffee down and started folding clothes. "That's real cute of you, defending him, but one night of sobriety doesn't set the record straight."

Ishmael rolled over. "I promise I'm not defending him."

"Well, is it going to be awkward when you see him?"

Diane seemed excited: like she wanted it to be awkward.

"I hope not. He's cooking me breakfast," Ishmael said.

Diane glanced over at Ishmael as she folded the clothes. "Well, then, what in tarnation are you doing back over here then?" She swatted Ishmael with the blouse in her hands. "Get up! Get out of here! If I were you—" She paused. "Well, let's just say I wouldn't be lounging around with a bunch of old hens waiting for that boy to get the syrup on the table!"

"Old hens and one rooster," Ishmael said. She propped a pillow behind her. "I wanted Allen to see me wake up in this bed so I could avoid another confrontation. I need to talk to him."

"Sugar, Allen already left."

"What—when?"

"Last night. Before supper even. He said he'd be back. But then he didn't come back. No messages on my cell phone. His is turned off." She looked away and added in a softer voice, "I saw him talk to you. I guess he was more upset than I thought. He must be on his way back to Cali."

"Well damn. What should I do?"

"Nothing," Diane said. "Go have breakfast with that stallion."

"But you leave tomorrow for Miami. You'll jump in a cab and drive off down that dirt road and I won't—"

"Everything is going to be just fine," Diane said, folding her clothes. "This is what you wanted, right? Allen to leave and go back to Cali without you."

Hector appeared in the doorway.

"Top of the morning." He looked around the room, suddenly aware that he had interrupted a moment. "Should I come back?"

"Heavens no! Come on in here, you darling sweet hunk of a man," Diane said, dispersing any tension.

"Nice to see such beautiful women in the guest room," he said. "Does wonders for the shoddy paint job in here."

Diane stood straighter and tilted her chin down. Her lips slid into a mischievous grin at the sight of Hector, but he had his sights solely on Ishmael.

"I missed you in my bed this morning," he said.

Ishmael was both embarrassed and flattered by this lack of inhibition.

"Yeah, I—" She shot a quick glance at Diane. "Had a bad dream."

"You should've woken me up," he said.

"Damn right, she should've. *I* would've woken you up, you good-looking angel." Diane turned to Ishmael. "Darling, you're probably just burning off all that damn stress you've been under lately."

"We should do a tarot card reading for you later," Hector said.

Ishmael looked up. "Are you joking?"

"Not at all. I draw from my deck almost every day."

"I've got to warn you, you may've just lowered your stock," Ishmael said.

"What's wrong with getting a little advice and perspective from universal wisdom now and then?" Hector asked.

Diane folded her clothes and looked curiously at Ishmael, anticipating with interest her reaction to this statement.

"I'm just not really into that sort of thing," Ishmael said.

"Last night, before you came over, I drew a card for you—*The Tower*. It's a major card. Do you know that one? Person falling from a tower?"

"Oh, I love dream interpretation!" Diane trilled, dropping the clothes she was folding in her suitcase and moving closer. "What's a major card? I've never heard of this. Is this like that gypsy woman stuff?" She sat on the bed. "I'm all ears, handsome."

"Can you do that? Draw a card for someone else?" Ishmael asked, but both Diane and Hector ignored her.

"It's not exactly dream interpretation," he said. "But when Ish said she had a bad dream, I remembered drawing that specific card. I had this quick vision. Figured that card might have something to do with her dream. Worth a shot."

"Damn straight." Diane turned to Ishmael. "Isn't this *fascinating*?"

Ishmael rolled her eyes.

With an audience, Hector continued. "*The Tower* card depicts a person falling off a tower into water with lightning bolts crashing all around. People think it's unlucky, but basically it just means that something in your life needs to shift. Like you're stuck. Stuck and stagnant. It's kind of a warning. Take charge, make a move or else, kind of thing."

"*Really?*" Diane said, her eyebrows lifting curiously. She shot a suspecting glare in Ishmael's direction. "Does that ring any bells, hon?"

"NO."

"Oh, don't get your panties in a clump. Live a little. Tell us about that dream of yours."

Ishmael had to admit; she was intrigued. She hadn't told Hector her nightmare was about falling.

"So what does it say to do?" Ishmael shuffled the sheets nervously. "I mean, *if* your life is stagnant?"

"Soul-searching," he said. "Make a move before the move makes you."

Ishmael pulled the covers off her. "Great. Just what I need. More deep reflection and life-altering changes."

"The card predicts you'll have a flash of insight," he said. "Guidance. Something'll happen to let you know what to do."

"There's the good news, sugar," Diane said, looking up from her suitcase briefly. "Don't you think so?"

"You two are cracking me up," Ishmael said, even while denying the interpretation, she found herself wondering.

"Pancakes are all ready," Hector said. "Banana pancakes with homemade pecan butter. Keeping them warm in the oven. You still coming over?"

Diane pressed her knuckles into her cocked hip.

"Get out of here and eat this man's pancakes."

Ishmael climbed from beneath the sheets, still dressed in Hector's clothes from the night before.

"For heaven's sake!" Diane dug through her suitcase. She held up a red dress. "Here, put this on."

"What? No way!" Ishmael said.

Diane turned to Hector. "Honey-pot, can you give us girls a little moment here?"

Hector bowed out of the doorway. "Be on the front steps."

Since the house was wide-open, Diane attempted a whisper. "A little loving can always put me in a good mood and give me a little clarity when I need it. After sex, I always seem to have a better perspective on things." Diane's voice returned to normal as she held out a shirt. "Here, how about this?"

"I'm going for pancakes. Not a date."

"Fine. That's your choice, Miss goody two-shoes, but I'm just telling you, some good loving might help."

Ishmael caught a glimpse of herself in the mirror and grabbed the shirt. She sighed, pulled Diane's shirt over her head, and looked back at herself in the mirror. She did look better.

"There, see, it fits perfect," Diane confirmed. "Now, how about those linen pants of mine with that shirt? I buy my pants long since I wear everything with heels." Diane went into the bathroom and returned pulling brushes and bottles out of a small case. "You want to shower first and use my gardenia soap?" Diane looked up and caught Ishmael's expression. "Okay, okay. Here—" Diane sprayed Ishmael with her perfume. "Now at least you smell nice."

Ishmael coughed at the potent mist.

"Okay—you're ready, GI Jane. Having no hair to fix sure does makes things go quicker, I'll give you that. Now get on out of here before I invite myself over for breakfast."

"You're welcome to join us," Ishmael said.

Diane batted her eyes. "Thank you, but *no way*. Besides, Lena promised to make me a shrimp omelet," she said, pushing Ishmael out the door.

Ishmael and Hector left the porch and headed across the lawn. Ishmael was pensive. Hector interrupted her worries.

"So I saw that nasty bruise on your leg when you slid out of bed this morning," he said as they walked. "Is that from the other night? From saving me?"

"You watched me get dressed this morning? I thought you were still asleep."

"I couldn't resist. It was torture to watch you go." Hector looked over at her. "I knew you had your reason for leaving so early. I can respect that."

Next thing, Hector had swooped Ishmael off her feet and into his arms. She pretended to fight and told Hector to put her down, but she didn't mean it.

"Look, if I'm the reason you got that bruise, I can't let you walk on that leg," he said.

Hector's flirtations certainly took her mind off her worries, off her nightmare, off the fact that she had broken Allen's heart and was ignoring her grandmother's warnings.

"You smell nice," he said.

She smiled back at him, resting her head wearily on his shoulder. There was no resisting him.

24

HE CARRIED HER INTO THE DOCK HOUSE and put her down on the couch. Hovering over her briefly, he leaned down and kissed her forehead before moving to the kitchen. The oven opened and soon he returned with plates stacked with pancakes.

"Hope you're cool with butter on your pancakes."

He poured fresh honey from a mason jar over the plates and handed her a fork. She put the first bite in her mouth.

"Here—ah, you got a little something on your—yep, there, that's got it." He handed her a napkin. "So I really am curious." He paused, cutting his first bite from the stack on his plate. "What's next in line for Ish Morgan?"

She put her fork down.

"I guess, when I really think about it, all this mermaid stuff just—it makes my heart flutter. And I can't tell whether that's because I'm freaked out or excited."

"Probably a bit of both," Hector said. "That's what's so amazing about all this. It's thrilling."

"Yeah, but I still have visions of getting married and having kids and selling my paintings, just putting this whole thing behind me. Living a normal life. Whatever *that* is."

Hector stopped chewing while she spoke.

"Are you serious?" he asked, eyebrows raised quizzically.

"Well, it's impossible anyway. I know too much. But I'm embarrassed to say I sometimes want to be shallow. There are times I'm actually jealous of people who can conform. I would love to just fall in line."

"Don't say that."

"Look, I know that I can't just put blinders on and act like none of this ever happened."

Hector set his plate down.

"I enjoyed last night, and don't get me wrong, I'm attracted to you, Hector, but in some strange way, I miss Nicholas." Ishmael paused, closing her eyes to focus, and then shook her head as she tried to think of the right words.

"You sure it's him you really miss?"

"Okay. Fine. *Honestly?* I miss the fact that I had it all planned out! Life was *easy*—secure—with him. I'd just go from one event to the next—dodging the mishaps, taking spa days when I got stressed, throwing money at any problems in my life! My most difficult decisions were choosing paint colors or deciding which bottle of wine to open."

"Could you honestly be happy with such a superficial existence?"

"I don't know. Maybe. I mean, I was. Kinda. Shoot, I mean—I guess I didn't understand how hard it would be to just pioneer a new path for myself. I guess the charted course just seems way easier."

"Of course the charted course is appealing right *now*. You're in the crux of a situation."

He picked up her plate of food and held it out to her.

"I'm not hungry anymore."

He set the plate back down.

"You're supposed to go the way you feel guided, Ish. The key is to listen to your gut."

"How did this all happen anyway?" she asked.

He stopped mid-bite, fork hovering.

"You came to South Carolina," he said. "We're attracted to each other."

"Not us. The whole mermaid thing. How's it possible? You've studied this stuff. Tell me about it. Maybe then I won't take it for granted."

"You're sure you want to know?" he asked. "Once I tell you the facts, you might be forced to believe them."

"I've seen my own tail," she said. "I just want to understand how."

He swept a final bite across his plate and then sat back, crossing his arms. He seemed defensive and protective of the story he was about to tell, but also seemingly desperate to talk about a subject so captivating to him.

"So there was this marine biologist named Alister Hardy. And he had this theory called the Aquatic Ape Hypothesis."

"Promising start. Keep it coming."

"So the theory goes that there was a drought. A major one. Lush forests turned to grasslands. And as the trees disappeared, the apes had nowhere to live and nowhere to hide, no real protection from predators. But the apes that made it to water—to the ocean— were the ones that were able to survive." He stood and poured hot water into a mug with a tea bag. "You want a cup?"

"I want to know how being in the water saved the apes."

He smiled.

"At the time of the drought, apes weren't comfortable with bipedalism—they mostly knuckle-walked on their fists and back feet—but their spines could at least handle standing on two legs. And the water helped them stabilize," he explained. "The apes that went to the water were spared because they could wade out into the water on two feet when they were chased by four-legged predators."

"Okay, so they escaped and didn't get eaten. I guess I'm having trouble understanding how apes became mermaids?"

"This is evolution we're talking about here, Ish. Didn't happen overnight. Happened over thousands of years."

"Yes, but I'm trying to figure out why there's an evolutionary line of humans that have fins instead of feet," she said. "They went to the water, but what made them stay?"

"Childbirth, most likely. They started birthing their babies in the water because it was safe. And then the apes started raising their young in the water to keep their offspring from being eaten. Whole clans of apes began to live in and near the water. There was no reason to leave. No trees to return to yet. And over millions of years—with a few mutations, genetic drift, things like that—evolution shifted the apes into fully aquatic creatures. But that last bit is where we venture away from Hardy's hypothesis. Hardy didn't say there were mermaids. He just used his theory to explain the human evolution on land."

"So how are there land humans and water humans?"

"Well, there were two branches of apes that escaped to the ocean. There were ones that became fully aquatic—those were the ones that chose to live *in* the water. But there was another cluster of apes that merely lived near the water. And they eventually went back into the savannas. But they left the water walking on two feet and with bigger brains thanks to diets heavy in fish oils. They weren't apes when thcy returned to the grasslands. They were the beginnings of humankind."

"And so thc first branch—the fully aquatic ones—became mermaids?"

"Essentially. They're what humans mistake for creatures that are half fish and half human." He looked at Ishmael. "But we're not fish—we're mammals. Just like humans—only the aquatic version."

Hector sipped from his mug, leaning against the counter, while Ishmael processed.

"What's more," he started, "if you take it even further back—and this part really blows my mind—our blood and the ocean share the same bicarbonate buffering system, a system that stabilizes and maintains proper pH. We both have this buffering system because the cells of our bodies were first derived, billions of years ago, in the sea. Do you comprehend how profound this is that the blood in our veins is so similar to the fluid of the ocean? Quite literally, it proves that we are children of the ocean."

"You're a total nerd. You know that?" she said.

He smiled, setting his mug down, and turned toward the sink to start the dishes.

Something caught his eye. He pulled the curtain aside, glancing out the window. He tapped his fist on the counter twice in quick succession.

"I knew she'd come," he said.

Without a glance Ishmael's way, he darted for the door. Frantically turning the knob, he ran out of the room.

25

ISHMAEL FOLLOWED HECTOR DOWN THE DOCK, running after him. "What's going on?"

Hector pointed to the crab pot stuffed full of pinching crabs. Water still dripped from the wire frame.

"What the—how'd the trap get so full?" she asked, admiring the vibrant blue crab legs with their orange-tipped claws.

"Get Maggie," Hector said. When Ishmael didn't move, he put his hands on her shoulders and yelled. "Ish! *Go!*"

She backed away from the intensity in Hector's eyes and sprinted up the dock. Once she was halfway across the lawn, she saw Maggie rushing off the screen porch.

"Hector told me—"

"I know—I saw the crab pot," Maggie said as she sped past. She crossed the lawn and then raced down the ramp to the floating dock with Ishmael in tow. "Is it her?" Maggie asked, out of breath.

Hector nodded. "Got to be. She's the only one who fills the trap before she puts it on the dock."

Ishmael's eyes shot to the water beneath the dock; there was nothing in the shadows. She recognized the sound of the screen door slamming and then heard Diane and Lena making their way across the lawn. She didn't dare turn to look—her eyes were focused on the water.

"I'm going in," Hector said. "With all three of you here, I might have a chance."

"Three of—what's going on?" Ishmael turned to Maggie. "Who's here?"

Hector dove into the water. Ishmael heard the splash and saw his clothes in a pile on the dock.

Diane was strutting down the dock in her high heels, pinning a sun hat to her head with one hand.

"Jesus-god-almighty! Am I dreaming or did that gorgeous thing just take his clothes off?"

Hector surfaced and paddled with his arms, allowing his legs to drag behind him while the others searched the creek for signs of the visitor. After only a minute, he leaned back in the water and lifted his legs: they were already beginning to bind.

"Ho—lee *shit*," he said, gazing at his legs. "It's much stronger this time." He looked at Maggie. "I could feel it as soon as I got in the water."

"What in the—" Diane was fanning herself with her sun hat, puffing like she was about to faint. She pointed. "So he's a—" She walked over to the bench. "I think I need to sit down for this one."

Maggie gaped at Hector's tail. "But we're not even in the water with you!"

"Apparently it doesn't matter," he said. "Just need all three of you nearby."

He dove beneath the surface. His partially formed fluke was

visible for a moment and then disappeared with him underwater. He resurfaced with a wide, elated smile and exhaled, sputtering water from his face. He turned back to the dock. "She's here, Maggie. It's definitely Anna."

"Anna?" Ishmael stepped forward. "My *mother*?"

A splash caused them all to spin around.

The female released a clean, gentle exhale as she broke the surface, her lids never blinking, even as the water dripped from her face. Her eyes were bright, her cheeks flushed with health. She was older, with the typical dreadlocked mane for hair, but she was larger and more exquisite than any of the other aquatic humans Ishmael had seen. Colorful feathers and exotic shells were woven into her tangles. The ornaments gave her hair the look of a headdress.

Lena crossed her arms over her chest. A knowing smile broke her face. "Mm-hm. Yes, ma'am. I knew this day would come. All the mommas and babies reunited."

Maggie contained her smile, but her eyes glinted with recognition.

"Only you could pull off an approach like that." Her words were like a peace offering. "Always impressive." She gestured across the dock with a nod of her chin. "And we're grateful for a full trap."

A slight smile back and the female nodded.

Lena lifted the crab pot with ease, admiring the contents. "Some good ones in here, too. We're gonna have us some crab cakes tonight thanks to you, Anna."

Ishmael turned to Maggie. Tears flooded her eyes. Maggie took her hand and nodded to the female in the water.

"It's my pleasure, Ishmael, to re-introduce you to your mother."

Diane whimpered from the bench. Lena pulled a handkerchief from her apron and handed it to her.

At Maggie's words, Anna looked Ishmael in the eyes, a deep loving stare. The corners of her lips curved up into a warm smile, and she tilted her head forward in a reverent bow. When she lifted her head again, Ishmael saw her own face reflected. She saw her sturdy jawline and high cheekbones. She saw her nose as if it had been taken from between her own eyes and sculpted onto this face before her. The wide-set bluish-gray eyes were the exact same color of her own.

"*Mom*?" She took a step closer.

"Ishmael, Anna doesn't speak anymore," Maggie said, resting a hand on Ishmael's shoulder. "She left that behind when—"

"Yah-ess. Mah-thur," Anna said. "Ish-may-elle. Daw-ter."

Ishmael covered her mouth with her hand, laughing and crying at the same time.

Maggie rested a hand on her chest. "Oh, Anna . . ."

Hector surfaced beside Anna and her smile broadened. The comparison of his broad shoulders emerging from the water next to Anna's made hers a touch more feminine. She pressed her forehead to his in a familiar greeting.

Hector lifted his tail, proud to show Anna. She patted the tail and chirped in congratulations. Her eyes portrayed her full awareness of the importance of this moment for him.

Hector dropped his tail and looked up at the dock. "Anna says it may take time to fully form. It can be a progression. But with all three of you, it could happen." He looked to Anna to make sure he was correct in his translation. Anna nodded. "She thinks eventually it will form completely. Then I'll be able to swim distance. Offshore even."

Maggie exhaled, bringing her hands to her heart. "Oh, that's marvelous news, Hector."

"Yeah," he said, "Apparently Ishmael's got the mojo, 'cause this never worked with just the two of you."

Anna kicked her fluke and raised her body almost completely out of the water. Gracefully balancing with her fluke, she held this raised position and pointed to her chest.

"Gaw," Anna said. "Gaw wih mah-thur."

Ishmael stood stunned.

Maggie stepped forward and put a hand on Ishmael's shoulder. "Your mother wants to take you with her."

Ishmael could see in her mother's eyes that Maggie's words were true. Her mother wanted to take her out to sea.

Diane stood from the bench and click-clacked in her stilettos across the dock toward Ishmael. Just as she was about to open her mouth, she remembered her manners and turned to Anna in the creek.

"Diane Dunaway," she said with a slight curtsy. She paused, obviously entranced by the sight of both Anna and Hector in the water. "It's a pleasure to . . . know Ishmael's—well, *goodness*—" She turned back to Maggie. "Can she even understand me?"

Anna kicked to lift herself out of the water. Diane drew in her breath as Anna tilted her head forward in a bow and then dropped back into the creek with barely a splash.

"I have *got* to get me one of those tails," Diane muttered. She turned back to Ishmael and Maggie. "Let me get this straight. You're telling me Ishmael's just supposed to dive off this dock and swim off into the Atlantic?" Her brow wrinkled. "Is that safe?"

"Anna will be with her," Maggie said. "She'll teach Ishmael everything there is to know about the ocean. There's no better guide than my daughter."

Ishmael looked from Diane to Maggie to Hector—then finally, to her mother.

"Wait—you guys think I should actually do this?" She turned to Maggie. "This is crazy!"

"Oh, hell yes, it's *crazy*," Diane said. She pointed to Anna in the water. "But look at her! Have you ever seen anything that amazing?" She rubbed Ishmael on the back. "And she's your *mother*, darling."

"It's not my mother I'm doubting," Ishmael said.

Hector kicked with his tail and held himself on the edge of the dock with his forearms.

"Ishmael Morgan," he said. "You know I don't want you to leave."

Ishmael felt a twinge of sadness. She glanced at her mother and then turned back to Hector. "Come with us," she said. She knew it was impulsive, but she meant it. She wanted him with her.

"There'd be no stopping me if it wasn't for this."

He lifted his partially formed fluke.

Shouldn't she stay here? With him? Help him progress his fluke to completion so they could swim off together?

"I can't keep you here," he said, shaking his head. "It's not fair. As much as I'd like to."

Ishmael knelt down beside him.

"Just know I feel the same about you," he said, seemingly reading her thoughts.

"But you won't be able to change without me. You won't be able to make progress."

"Who knows how long my process will take? It could take weeks for me to fully transform. Months, even. This is your mother, Ish. Go with her."

His smile seemed forced, but she appreciated his selflessness.

"I promise I won't let this be the last time we see each other," she vowed.

"We're all gonna need safety goggles if you two don't stop!" Diane was fanning herself with her hat. "Chemistry between you two—Damnation, this better *not* be the last time!"

Ishmael pushed back up to standing, her face flushing red.

Maggie walked across the dock and held Ishmael's cheeks in her hands, gazing deep into her granddaughter's eyes before she kissed her on the forehead and shifted her gaze back to the creek.

"I know you'll take good care of her, Anna. I'm so proud of both of you."

Anna chirped in response just before she sunk beneath the surface. Ishmael could barely see in the murky water, but she watched her mother contort her body in a turn and then kick with her powerful silver tail, swimming away.

"Wait! Now? Just like that! I'm just supposed to dive in and follow her?"

Maggie wrapped her arms around Ishmael and squeezed her tightly.

"No time like the present," Maggie said.

Ishmael looked to her grandmother and found confidence in the wise eyes that unflinchingly stared back. She turned back to the water, feeling a slight breeze brush her face. She smiled, peeling off her clothes.

Ishmael stood on the dock, the wind swirling across her naked flesh. What the hell was she doing? She wasn't sure. And, yes, she was afraid. But then—this was her mother. She was drawn to her and to the ocean with a powerful, almost irresistible force.

She took a deep breath in anticipation of her plunge. Suddenly this wasn't just a creek she was diving into; it was another realm, another dimension.

She shook her head in disbelief and dove off the dock.

EPILOGUE

THE OCEAN SWALLOWED ME WHOLE. No biting, no chewing. I simply slid down her throat and became a part of her.

Imagine this: a puff of breath, an exhale so tension-free that it's expelled with the soft force of a draft lifting a curtain. This is my new trained efficiency.

I dive and see hundreds of tiny iridescent fish moving as one unit, stretching and morphing like an amoeba. I dart through the center of their wobbly sphere, parting the cluster like a drapery for a brief pause before they close behind me.

Eyes open underwater, I spiral through the sea, driven by the power of my rippling lower half. At my side, birds plummet with dramatic splashes, hefty tunas thrust with lightning speed to gulp shiny flickers of fish. Trained by my mother, I too pluck these fish for nourishment as easily as if I am gathering ripe tomatoes from a garden.

I might worry that my mother is taking me on a swim across the Atlantic Ocean—to Bermuda, I'm supposing—but her skill and resourcefulness placate any apprehensions. I can now detect the subtle differences between the nectar of tuna, the oiliness of flying fish, and the chewy slip of squid.

I live in a world of cobalt blue, devoid of all green: the color of the crayon a child would select to draw the sea on a clean white piece of paper. I am a single totem in the center of a flowing stampede of porpoises. I drink fresh water squeezed from a cloud. I dream sweetly through the darkness of night on the softness of my ocean waterbed.

I am hidden, but I hope you will still look for me. I am out there.

Acknowledgments

Boundless gratitude for the friends who started this process with me and read my first unedited and sloppy drafts: Joan Algar, Dr. Bill Slayton, Melissa McConnell, Barbara Villasenor of First Reads, and Farrar Hood Cusomato. Without each of them, I probably would have given up when I realized what a significant undertaking this was going to be. My profound appreciation goes out to my editors, Renni Browne and Shannon Roberts of The Editorial Department. These two women pushed me to my limits and I remain in awe and humble appreciation for the remarkable transformation that occurred under their years of guidance. I want to also thank my sisters, Anna Smith and Ellen Mostellar, who were my final, finishing-touches editors. I feel our uniqueness combined with our bond of sisterhood made us an extraordinary editorial team. In particular, Ellie's encouragement and patient advice were my treasures in the concluding stages of this journey. I know I wouldn't have made it across the finish line without her. Shiva the Chocolate Labrador Retriever sat under my desk and was my loyal writing companion. Thanks to her adamancy for walks, I took much-needed breaks from the computer to swim in a creek or hike on a trail. I love and miss my companion every day. My old friend Charles Ailstock, with whom I attended kindergarten, gets an enormous shout-out for creating the woodcut portrait of Ishmael (illustration on the cover). He took my description of Ishmael and so flawlessly brought the words to life with his art. Elaine Morgan, whom I never had the privilege of meeting in this lifetime, wrote the books on anthropology, evolution, and feminism that I devoured in the beginning stages of this manuscript. Her bold spunk to question established conventions and her passionate grit to announce her heartfelt truth will eternally inspire me.

I give the biggest thank you of all to my husband, Legare, who selflessly bolstered my every stroke along this writing odyssey. He is the reason this book came to fruition. So many times when I was drowning in a sea of self-doubt, he captained me. Legare, with all my heart, I thank you.

And to Ishmael, wherever you are, thanks for whispering your story in my ear.

About the Author

Kate Smith was born and raised in Charleston, South Carolina and has spent a significant portion of her adult life living on the West Coast. She now resides in the Deep South on the shores of the Atlantic Ocean with her boat captain husband and their two water-loving, brown dogs. She owns a yoga studio named after Mother Earth.

31901059796203